THE
KALI
CONNECTION

A Lynn Evans Mystery
by
Claudia McKay

New Victoria Publishers Inc.

Published by New Victoria Publishers, Inc. PO Box 27 Norwich Vermont, a feminist, literary and cultural organization founded in 1976.

Cover design by Ginger Bown
Cover Painting by Sakotha Tole
Printed on recycled paper

ISBN 0-934678-54-5

Library of Congress Cataloging-in-Publication Data

McKay, Claudia.
    The Kali connection / by Claudia McKay.
        p.   cm.
    "A Lynn Evans mystery."
    ISBN 0-934678-54-5 : $9.95
    1. Women journalists--Nepal--Fiction. 2. Smuggling--Nepal-
-Fiction.. 3. Lesbians--Nepal--Fiction.   I. Title'.
PS3563.C3734K34   1994
813'.54--dc20
                                                            93-42942
                                                            CIP

To Nepal's poet, novelist, revolutionary and feminist,
Bishnu Kumari Waiba Parijat—1936-1993

1

Warm spring rain spattered the leather of Lynn's camera
case as she ran the few blocks from her office at the *Chroni-cle* to the old Emery Hotel in downtown Hartfield to check out
what might be a drug-related suicide.

She had been about to leave the office early to enjoy the last
of a fine spring day, maybe even take the time to sit on a park
bench and watch the sunset, when her boss, Gale Donahue had
sent her on this assignment.

Tucking her camera under the jacket that hung loosely over
her spare frame, she brushed damp, frizzy, sun-bleached hair
back from her forehead. How ironic that now, too late, she was
trying to slow her life down as Shirley had wanted, taking more
time to enjoy the little things around her. Lynn still couldn't
think about Shirley's good-bye note—*You're married to your
newspaper. What do you need me for?*—without feeling sad. Yet
in some ways she was glad Shirl had left. It simplified her life—
no more hassles over late hours—no more constant analysis of
their relationship over endless cups of coffee—no more worry
about last minute assignments that would ruin their plans.

After all, being a reporter meant you were always on call.
And it was raining, so there wouldn't be much of a sunset anyway. Lately even the small things weren't turning out right.

Outside the hotel, people were standing in the street peering
through narrow dirty windows. Lynn pushed her way inside,
camera in hand. Built in the last century, the Emery was high-
ceilinged and pretentious in spite of its dowdiness. There was
just one first-floor hallway beyond the registration desk and
front stairway. What space was left for the lobby—crammed
between the staircase and the dusty, street-front windows—was

full of onlookers clustered around one couch and a coffee table. The lace doily under the straggly geranium in the window looked as if it had been last washed and ironed during the Depression. The couch, covered with a clear plastic wrap, looked newer.

Lynn braced herself against a window ledge to get a clearer view for pictures. Already the police had cordoned off the area with yellow tape, and were measuring and photographing. The tape around the stairway left just enough room for the tenants to get past the desk and down the narrow hall. The ancient elevator beyond the front desk and next to the staircase bore a sign—Out of Order.

The body of a youngish man sprawled awkwardly half-way down the stairs, one arm around a wooden banister post as if he had tried to grab it to break his fall. Longish dark hair almost covered his pale face with its day's growth of beard. He was wearing white pajamas, or was it some type of martial arts outfit? And no shoes. There was some sort of mark on his neck. Had it happened when he fell?

Were those spots of blood on his shirt and dotting the stair treads? Lynn put a lens on her camera for a closer look. They were red flower petals, geranium probably. She noticed something draped over the man's left hand—what looked like the remains of a shallow basket with a few more red petals in it. More petals were strewn across the floor and stairs.

After taking some photos, she turned on her tape recorder and pushed closer. Crime scenes were usually too noisy to get much on tape without sticking a mike in somebody's face, but sometimes off-the-cuff remarks came through.

The police officer in charge came down the stairs and told the crowd to clear a passageway. It was Detective Roger Thomas. So she was in luck after all. Thomas and his partner Del Whitney were friends of hers. At least Del was, and Thomas put up with her almost amicably.

The crowd reluctantly moved back. Lynn moved closer holding up the mike for her tape recorder. "How'd it happen Detective Thomas? Another drug overdose?"

He squatted down near some red petals. "An overdose of drugs is the apparent cause of death. Won't know for sure till more lab tests come in."

"Have you identified the victim?"

"The register lists him as Sam Jenson. An unemployed sales-man—did some labor jobs around. According to the neighbors an ex-drug addict."

"Did he phone for help? "

Thomas shook his head. "Desk clerk called. Jenson was already dead by the time we got here." He stood up and said in a louder voice, "You folks will have to stand back. Please step out-side unless you are a resident of this hotel."

A uniformed cop moved forward to encourage the onlookers to leave. Lynn went to the hotel's registration desk where a bald-ing clerk was leaning over the scarred counter top to get a better view through his bifocals. "You the one that called the police?" she asked as she took more photos. She often got more out of people if they thought they might get their picture in the paper.

"Naw, Nelson was on duty. Called me in so he could go down-town to make a statement."

"Do you know what happened... Mr...?"

He squinted at her through his thick glasses. "Beck's the name, George Beck. Whadya expect from these hippie types. Nelson saw him come staggering downstairs. He called the med-ics and the cops, but he figured the guy would be dead by the time anybody got here."

"How'd he know?"

George Beck shrugged. "Seen enough of 'em I guess."

"Did you know the dead man?"

George frowned. "He's lived here a few years. I don't usually work days so I don't get to know the regulars so well, but he liked to talk. Good to jaw with sometimes on night shift. Helped pass the time. He was good company in the old days. Hasn't been around recently though. Got into some eastern cult crap. Lately he quit eating meat, quit drinking, practically quit talk-ing, quit just about everything. Hadn't been working many hours anyway. Sat around all the time in his room meditating or something when he wasn't out at their mission or something."

"Do you know the name of the group?"

He shrugged. "Naw. They're all the same. You know, funny clothes, weird talk."

"Did he have friends—a girlfriend?"

"Pretty much a loner until he got in with them religious types."

"Any visitors lately?"

"Oh sure." The man's eyes narrowed. "A woman—pretty, dark—wore jingle jangles." He wiggled his arms to indicate bracelets. "I figured maybe she was why he got in with them spiritual types. She never stayed over though. Not on my shift anyway."

"You know her name?"

He frowned. "Mary...Marsha, something like that."

"What was Sam's room number?"

"You a cop?"

"I write for the paper. Investigative reporting."

"Room 302 on the third floor. The cops are still up there."

Thomas came up behind her. "I can't wait to read tomorrow's edition so I can solve this case," he said dryly.

Lynn saluted. "I can file a report if you want, Chief."

Thomas didn't laugh. Instead he began to question the clerk. "Tell me what you know about the deceased?" George began to repeat his story.

Lynn slipped past Thomas toward the elevator. It was one of the old-fashioned kind, a cage inside a sliding door, all wrought iron and wood; the out of order sign was scrawled on a page of the registration book in magic marker.

The clerk called to her. "Got to get it fixed. There are back stairs down the hall." She hurried down the hallway before Thomas could stop her.

A uniformed cop was standing at the bottom of the back stairs. She hadn't seen him before—good, he wouldn't spot her as an outsider. "Room four-forty-three, fourth floor," she said as she went past him with her camera under her jacket, hoping there were actually four habitable floors in the building. He didn't stop her.

The stairs were obviously rarely used. They were unswept and cluttered with mops, boxes and trash. The door to the third floor was ajar, though partially blocked by a carton of old rags. Being agile and slender, it was just possible for Lynn to slip past without touching anything or disturbing the box.

4

The door to room 302 was open with yellow tape across it. Lynn leaned in and took some shots. When the cops inside ignored her, she slipped casually over the tape and went on photographing without interference.

Sam Jenson had been neat; there wasn't the usual dust and clutter of a bachelor's apartment. A newish TV and VCR sat in one corner. The TV screen was turned toward the wall. Very curious. The desk clerk, Beck, had said the dead man had recently joined some sort of cult. Had Sam given up TV as part of some sort of religious austerity program? She looked into an open closet—a lot of expensive clothing, yet Beck had said he was unemployed.

Just as neat, on a clean towel laid out on an end table next to a small gray nylon bag, was some drug paraphernalia, a hypodermic needle, a small bottle of bleach, a few small cotton balls, a package of dime store balloons, a bottle of clear liquid, and a necktie.

Above the table was a cloth painting of a goddess; not one of those cheap prints, reproductions of sacred paintings done for the mass market, but a carefully executed original painting with exquisite detail. An Eastern goddess, four arms and a greenish face. On a shelf under the picture were a few scattered red flower petals and a partly burned candle. Had Sam been putting the small basket with an offering of flowers now clutched in his hands on this altar when...?

Lynn was still taking pictures when Thomas said from the doorway, "Gentlemen, let me introduce Ms. Lynn Evans, investigative reporter for the *Chronicle*."

The cops looked flustered and Lynn said, "Just going boss," and smiled at him as she stepped back out of the room. "Oh, by the way, the back door to this floor was ajar. I left the box of rags where I found it when I came through. I didn't touch anything." She saw Thomas flush but he didn't say anything.

In the hall Lynn noticed an older woman peeking out her door. Before she had a chance to duck back inside Lynn called out, "Ma'am, wait, may I speak to you for a moment?"

As she moved closer she held out her hand. "Lynn Evans, reporter from the *Chronicle*. And you are?"

The woman said shyly, "McCurdy, Myrtle McCurdy."

"Did you know Sam?"

5

The door opened a bit more. "He was a sweet boy, no matter what they say. Always polite and helpful, quiet.... It was that woman's fault that he got so different lately. Talking about spirits—Goddesses and such. Very unchristian if I do say so. I'll bet she poisoned him."

Lynn mulled over that one for a second. "Goddesses?—you mean like the one in the picture above Sam's altar?"

"That ugly green witch. It's obscene the way he went on about her—said she was his inspiration."

"You mean the green goddess?"

No. The woman of course, Marta, Marta Handley I think."

"The one you think poisoned him. Have you told the police what you think about her?"

The woman shook her head. There was suspicion and fear in her eyes now.

"I'd like to know more. May I come in? I'd like to interview you."

Myrtle started to close the door again.

Lynn blocked the door gently with her toe and deftly clicked on the small tape recorder now hidden in her pocket. "Just a personal interview of you. We will print only what you want us to. A few pictures...just your point of view."

A slight flush came to Myrtle's pale cheeks. "Well, I have to comb my hair if you're going to take pictures." Lynn smiled and Myrtle adjusted her dress. "Come on in then."

While Myrtle fussed in front of a mirror, Lynn stepped into a drab room, much the same size as Sam's, but more cluttered with knickknacks and furniture.

"Do you know where she can be found?"

Myrtle ran a brush through her hair. "Who?"

"The woman that you think poisoned Sam."

"Marta. She's a high mucky-muck in that group Sam was involved with. Sam said they have offices on Fourteenth Street but she mostly hangs out at their mission downtown."

"Why do you think she poisoned him?"

"All those people take drugs, don't they?"

"Not necessarily."

"She poisoned his mind, anyway. At least he didn't sleep with her. She didn't ever stay over; he always sent her away. He was a sweet boy, though I never thought much of his friends. But he wasn't very neat; his room was always a mess. He used to give me a little bit each week to clean up for him on Mondays. He knew I needed it to help stretch my pension."

"Did you clean for him recently?"

She frowned. "I haven't been in there in two months. He quit his job, for those cult people you see, poor boy."

"What did he do before?"

She shrugged. "Some sort of salesman I think. Dressed nice you know, respectable."

"What were his friends like? The ones you didn't like."

"I didn't like any of them. He was too good for them. I didn't like the ones from before the cult thing either. Some of them were sort of mean—to me anyway—rude."

"Have they been around lately?"

"Wednesday some of them came by, but he didn't even open the door when they banged on it. I told them he wasn't there. I was tired of their banging." She sat down on the bed opposite Lynn shaking her head. "Such a tragedy—so polite and helpful—he used to carry my groceries up the stairs."

Lynn took a few photos of Myrtle. "Did Sam have family?"

"He never mentioned anybody—blood relatives I mean. After he got involved with them he talked nonsense all the time—about how they were his family now."

"Who exactly are they?"

"Kalimaya, I think he said. Kalimaya Society."

Lynn remembered a previous *Chronicle* series on 'Post New Age' cults. Harmless enough as far as she knew. In any event, Kalimaya wasn't high profile like the Hare Krishnas, accosting people at airports, or Moonies, selling flowers door to door. She couldn't remember the name of the guru.

"This Marta—do you know anything about her?" Lynn ask.

"Certainly not." Myrtle said a bit huffily.

"Did Sam seem particularly upset or worried lately?"

"It wasn't suicide if that's what you're thinking. He said weird stuff, but he was a happy boy recently—I'll have to say that much. Very pleased with himself and his new life style as he put it."

"Are you saying you think it was murder?"

7

Myrtle's eyes narrowed as if in the realization that she might have said too much and she snapped, "Don't you quote me on that. All I said is he seemed happy."

Lynn decided not to press the point, giving her a quick, reassuring smile. Then she asked Myrtle a few questions about herself, took a couple more shots of the woman among her collection of tea cups and hurried out.

Back in the lobby she discovered a repair man already working on the elevator. To her question he answered, "A hunk of metal is missing from the cage. Door won't close."

"You think somebody broke it deliberately?"

He laughed. "This thing is so old it quits all the time. Should have been replaced long ago. Broke more often than fixed."

"What happened to the section of metal?"

He shrugged. "Might have fallen down the shaft. Can't be put back anyway. I'll have to make a piece—put it on with bolts."

She hurried to find Thomas to see if he had sent anyone to the bottom of the elevator shaft, and found him surrounded by reporters. She stood for a while on the fringe, but knew she would get more with a phone call later when Thomas was less distracted. Since his partner Del Whitney was conspicuously absent—presumably out gathering information—they must be assuming more to this case than suicide, much like Myrtle had.

At that moment Del came hurrying through the front door, usual tweed jacket, dark hair cut close, big gold earrings against mahogany, silk-smooth skin. If that woman wasn't straight....

Lynn went to meet her. It was one of the few times she could recall seeing Del out of breath as she said, "Would you believe I got caught in a traffic jam? I parked—faster to run here than drive." She glanced at Thomas fielding questions from some other press people who had just arrived. "Fill me in, Lynn," Del said, frowning, "that other desk clerk wasn't much help."

Lynn told her what Myrtle had said and then pulled her toward the elevator. "I want you to look at something." She pointed out the missing metal on the cage and left Del talking to the repairman while she went on down the hall to the back entrance to check out the alley. Fortunately the policeman was no longer guarding the back stairs. That meant they had taken all the fingerprints they were going to take.

8

The back door had two locks but the safety catch was off. The knob had a self-lock that opened from the inside not the outside. She went into an alley which ended to the right in another building with bricked up windows, two stories up. A locked door of another old brick building was opposite the hotel. The alley stank, garbage cans overflowing. At the left end of the alley a broken couch blocked the way out, no doubt waiting for the trash truck. A slight movement caught her eye and she moved toward that end of the alley. A man covered with corrugated cardboard was asleep or passed out on the couch. Lynn tried to shake him awake, and he brushed her away, but then reached for the dollar that she waved in his face. She pulled it away and gestured toward the hotel. "You see anybody today—coming out of this building?" He grabbed the bill, shook his head, and then shut his eyes.

Lynn sat gingerly on the edge of the lumpy cushion. "Come on. You can talk to me. I'm not a cop."

He looked at her and her camera bag, but didn't say anything for a long time. She pulled out a five, but kept it out of reach.

His voice was a husky whisper. "People come out sometimes to put out garbage."

"You saw someone this afternoon?"

"I been asleep." He closed his eyes again. She brought the five closer. He didn't open his eyes. "A guy climbed over me a while ago."

"How long ago?"

He glanced up at the sky and shrugged. "An hour maybe."

"What did this guy look like?"

"I don't know."

"How'd you even know it was a guy then?"

"He was big, noisy. Had on these cowboy boots. You know, with the fancy pattern on the pointy toes."

"You saw the boots?"

"Nearly stepped on me."

"What was he wearing?"

"Gray pants, some sort of flowered shirt. Hawaii print or something. My eyes aren't so good anymore."

"What about his hair, his face?"

He squinted, gauging the distance of the money.

9

Lynn stood up to take a picture of him. He frantically pulled the cardboard over his head. "No pictures in the paper, lady. I don't want social workers on my tail." One hand came out from under the cardboard. She put the five in it. He re-emerged slowly, watching to see if she had put the camera away. She screwed on the lens cap.

He said, "Sun was in my eyes—but I think the guy had kind of white or blondish hair, maybe gray—and a long plain face."

"Would you recognize him again?" Del had found Lynn out in the alley and moved up beside her.

"Shit, you said you weren't a cop."

"I'm not," Lynn answered. "This is Detective Delia Whitney. She just wants to ask you some questions. You might have seen a murderer, someone who might just come back after you."

"Shit...."

Del took over. "You see anybody else? "

"No, just Cowboy Boots. I think he didn't even know I was here—in too big a hurry."

"Where'd he go?"

"How should I know? Down the street."

Del sighed. "Hey, maybe it was you killed the guy for booze money."

"Yeah, sure...and I'd still be here." He looked at Lynn. "You didn't tell me there was a murder. That's worth at least ten bucks."

Lynn pulled out the money.

Del said, "He'll just kill himself with booze."

He sat up wearily. "Don't talk about me like I wasn't here. I hate that. I'm not stupid. I know how to pace myself—if I don't get robbed."

"We'll keep you safe."

"You arresting me?"

"Just some protective custody for a couple of days. Look at some pictures...unless you'd like to be the next victim."

"Bailey, my name's L.E. Bailey, but don't print that. Come on, the guy didn't even know I was here, and I couldn't pick him out for sure anyway."

"Well just in case, we'd like you to look at some photographs for us, Mr. Bailey." Del said politely.

Bailey snickered as if something she said was funny, but then he got up wearily and Del led him off gently. Lynn returned to the hotel.

In the hallway she ran into Thomas again. He said, grudgingly, "I know you'll give me a copy of the interview you taped of Mrs. McCurdy."

Lynn nodded."She seems to think Sam Jenson was not suicidal."

Thomas nodded. "I think I agree with her. The bag and contents matched up with earlier police reports on him; it was his stuff. He could have had a druggie's relapse. But I think he would have done a better job; the new needle marks are in a different place from the old scars. Clumsy job too."

"What about the head wound?"

"Might have fallen into the banister coming down the stairs."

"Anybody with a motive?"

"According to the desk clerk who found him, the last person to visit him was a woman named Marta Handley, a member of the Kalimaya Society. Not a likely candidate since she was the one to get him on the straight and narrow, but I think the Kalimayas warrant some looking into. Maybe Ms. Handley has a boyfriend that didn't like her visiting Sam."

"Somebody could have come in this back door—if it was left open."

Thomas shrugged. "Hell, maybe one of the other residents didn't like the way he wrapped his garbage." He pulled the pencil out from behind his ear. "There are still lots of things we don't know, although he's lived in this hotel a long time. We don't know how he made a living...except for a few odd jobs. Some people here think he might have had a record, some people didn't like his friends. Some people thought he had gone crazy in a religious cult and was killed in some kind of bizarre ritual. So what did the old lady have to say?"

"Sam liked his new religious lifestyle. He was polite, helped her with groceries, paid her to clean up for him Mondays."

Thomas drummed the pencil impatiently against his thumb, waiting.

"Myrtle said Sam had some friends she thought were rather rude, who, incidentally, tried to contact him last Wednesday and

11

were very unhappy when she told them he was out. I'm sure she could identify them. She didn't like his new religious family either. She thinks Marta Handley poisoned him."

Thomas grunted noncommittally and walked away.

Lynn went back to her office at the *Chronicle* to work up her story. Her editor wouldn't be too excited about the news report she turned in, but maybe Gale would let her do some follow up. Was there a connection between Sam's drug habit and the cult? The new suits in Sam's closet didn't fit with an out of work salesman. She was curious about the cult angle and wanted to look into that one for an in-depth article. Also, she would have to follow up on this Marta Handley.

• • •

The next day, first thing, Lynn called Del and asked, "Anything new?"

"No sign of Bailey's cowboy yet. Nobody else saw him."

"Anybody could have gotten out the back door without being seen."

"Anyway, one of the desk clerks and Myrtle identified a couple of guys that turned out to have been involved in the drug trade, but we haven't located them yet. "

"His woman friend, the Kalimaya devotee, Marta—her fingerprints are all over the apartment. Even on some of the drug stuff. Doesn't look good for her. Marta says she cleaned up the place for him sometimes, but was out giving away pamphlets all afternoon. No doubt her fellow cult members will supply an alibi."

Lynn was intrigued. It sounded as if Del was convinced Sam had been murdered. "What does Marta say about the drug paraphernalia?"

"Said she took the stuff away from Sam weeks ago to help him clean up. Threw it in the trash. Somebody else could have pulled it out and saved it of course. But they would have had to plan it for a long time. "

"Unless he pulled it out himself."

"Possible."

"A deliberate overdose?" Lynn asked

"Sure looks like it. He'd been off a long time, but he was too street smart not to know the dose. And there is the blow to the head. We don't think he did it falling down the stairs. Hitting the banister or a stair tread wouldn't have done that kind of damage, though it probably wasn't what killed him."

"He got down the stairs."

"Must have come to before the drug took over and tried to get help—too late, although somebody could have dropped him down unconscious to make it look like an accident."

"Maybe I'll look up this Marta—interview her."

Del sighed. "I suppose there is no point in asking you to lay off this one for a few days, Lynn."

"Just a personal interview about the Kalimaya Society. I'm curious. He had quite a goddess painting in his apartment—of Kali, I presume."

Del laughed. "That was a green Tara. A Buddhist saint, one of Buddha's wives some people say."

"I want to know what this Marta does, how they recruit and all. What their line is. These cults are always looking for good publicity—"

"All right, all right, go ahead," Del said wearily. "She'll be recruiting out by the Lindley Mall, you know that new little park, Gramercy. Just keep me informed, okay?"

She knew the place—more like Gramercy 'Parklet', because it was hardly more than a triangular piece of lawn surrounded by a few ill-placed, cement benches, the kind you wouldn't bother digging up and hauling away.

2

*L*indley Mall was in an upscale part of the city, a new shopping mall surrounded by condominiums retrieved from old brick and steel warehouses.

In the middle of the triangular lawn that passed for Gramercy park was what appeared at first to be a colorful circus act—a collection of acrobats and jugglers, dressed in loose, colorful, tie-dyed outfits—long shirts and baggy Eastern-style pants. They were being watched by a few shoppers surrounded by their purchases, a jogger running in place and a few older people sitting on the cement benches.

So, this was how they spread the word? Looked more like earnest young people just trying to make a little money, all before the encroaching rain closed the act. A piece about them ordinarily would barely make it to page twenty-eight, near the movie ads and theater reviews.

As she got closer she could see in the center of the crowd a youngish man with a shaved head and colorful clothing, juggling. Several other people, also theatrically dressed, handed out glossy pamphlets. Lynn quickly snapped a few pictures of the group then watched for a few moments to figure out who was in charge.

A graceful dark-haired woman in a full skirt, decorated with mirrors and bangles, and wrapped in a peacock blue silk shawl moved between the performers and the audience with pamphlets, encouraging one with a word, another with a smile. Lynn walked over to accept the booklet from her slim brown fingers and fell into deep brown eyes. She guessed from Del's description that this must be Marta.

"Thank you for allowing us to share the knowledge of our

path with you," floated from between Marta's smiling coral lips. Her quiet voice was steady, self confident. "If you will just take the time to read this..." The woman left her standing there to approach some shoppers walking by. Lynn looked down obediently at the pamphlet in her hand searching for something to say to start a conversation. She thumbed through the pages. It wasn't hard to find the kind of passage she expected:

Woman, due to her simpler nature, must follow man... Then further on: *If she is true to the way provided her she can gain access to the gate and enter the outer edges of heaven in order to serve there as she did on this earth...*

Lynn followed Marta and stood near her until she could look once again into the depths of her electric brown eyes. She asked, pointing to the passage, "You don't really accept this sort of thing as a necessary truth, do you?"

The woman didn't even read the passage. She just noted the page number and then said patiently, "Woman is one of the states of being on the path. It is our Karma."

Lynn took a deep breath. It always amazed her that women who seemed like they were perfectly intelligent couldn't see the oppressiveness of such traditional rhetoric. She couldn't suppress the bite behind her words. "You mean that if I am a good girl in this life, I might get to be an equal next time around? Or is it that I'll get to be a man then?"

Marta's complacent expression did not change, but she pulled her shawl tighter around her shoulders. "All must find their own path. We only hope to share our knowledge." A drop of rain dared to make a trail down her satin cheek.

The crowd began to disperse. If she was going to get an interview she should stop being so critical. "I'm not trying to insult you. I really would like to talk to you. I certainly have my doubts about Western patriarchal modes of thought. Perhaps we could go for coffee out of the rain. There's a place down the street that also has herb teas."

Marta shook her head and smiled. She handed Lynn a card. Under a large embossed eye Lynn read:

The Kalimaya society teaches the enlightened world view. Our work is based on ancient books of Eastern Wisdom.

At the bottom there was an address.

15

"Come to the mission and we can talk," Marta said.

Lynn quickly handed Marta her own card. The brown eyes read it and then probed her again. "Lynn Evans. So you are a newspaper reporter, another of the professional skeptics."

"Not always."

The smile faded. "The media hasn't treated us very well."

"We aren't always the bad guys. We can sometimes give you good press. Just let me talk to you...about my doubts if you like. An official interview with your leader can come later if you agree."

Worry lines still marred the smooth forehead, but the woman said, "I'm Marta Handley. Let's go get that cup of tea."

The muscular, blond, young man who had been juggling for the crowd came up to them shaking an offering bucket. He put a proprietary hand on Marta's arm and said to Lynn, "The Sister will be at the Thursday night meeting. Our address is there on the back of that pamphlet."

Marta frowned, but said nothing.

Lynn handed him her card. "Marta has agreed to talk to me."

The juggler frowned. "Come to a meeting. You can learn anything we want you to know there."

Marta still did not move. Was she really going to let him tell her what to do?

With what she hoped was an air of disinterested contempt, Lynn threw the change from her pocket into the bucket the juggler was holding. She couldn't help saying to Marta, "I can't see anything unusual about this group. It's certainly clear who has the power."

The juggler put an arm around Marta's shoulders persuasively. "Let's not stand here in the rain. We need to get our materials under cover."

Marta surprised Lynn by pulling away from him and saying, "You have enough hands to get that done. I'll find my own way back to the house." She and Lynn hurried away.

Seated in the little cafe with the rain beating against the window nearby, they smiled at each other over steaming cups of herb tea. Lynn suddenly realized how attracted she was to this woman. As the intense brown eyes studied her, she wondered how to interpret Marta's small rebellion. Had it been a lovers' disagreement? Had Marta just come with her because she wanted to recruit Lynn to the cult, or were those brown eyes really flirting with her?

As if to answer that question Marta said, "Jason is a good friend, but like many Western men, he sometimes forgets that he was not born to have power over others."

"Eastern men are different?"

Marta sighed. "It's a hard lesson for us all. Our Sister says that the only true empowerment is service. It's always hard not to expect a return for one's efforts. The Sister says there is no infinite balance sheet somewhere in the universe where it's recorded that we are owed gratitude or loyalty or love or even material reward."

She placed her hand over Lynn's. "She tells us that we must be even more tolerant of the males of our species because history has led them to believe that they are superior to us. That's why she does not edit the passages you object to but uses them as a way to teach us wisdom."

Lynn could feel herself flush at Marta's touch. Why hadn't she been born with lovely olive-brown skin like Marta's instead of her pasty pink skin that showed every emotion and wrinkle. She pulled away her hand and asked, "If religious thought contains so much wisdom, why are people always killing each other over religious principles?"

Marta looked down at her steaming cup and was silent for a moment. Then the brown eyes searched Lynn's once again. "I'm trying to understand that."

"Do you believe that your group has the answer?"

"I don't know yet. It's hard to get beyond the struggles of everyday survival. That's why you find us as a street carnival rather than contemplating important ideas on a mountain top."

"Would you rather be on a mountain top?"

"It sounds as if you have already begun an interview. I am not officially authorized to speak for The Kalimaya Society to the press."

"Unofficially then. I won't print it unless you give us the go-ahead."

Marta sighed, her face showing her tiredness now. "You said

you wanted to talk about your doubts. Was that really a ploy to get me to talk to you?"

Lynn thought for a minute. What was the truth? Of course she'd come to write about the Kalimayas because of Sam's involvement. She knew that Marta had already been questioned by the police so knew about his death. Mentioning it now would surely put the woman on the defensive, which was the last thing that Lynn wanted right now

She had always been intrigued by cults and neo-religious groups. What was it that was so seductive to people like Marta in spite of all the obvious pitfalls? Maybe it did make a difference that the spiritual leader was a woman. The truth, at least about her interest in cults like this one, was perhaps the right tack. "I do have doubts—both about the existence of the supernatural and about the role groups like yours play in our society."

Marta looked into her tea, stirring slowly. "So what do you want from me?"

"Who you are? What is your mission? With what other groups are you affiliated?"

Marta smiled and held up her hand. "No personal doubt now? No questions about your own life patterns? You are perfectly happy and satisfied. This is to be just an interview about us after all?"

Lynn felt herself closing up. She didn't care for the prospect of a conversion lecture. Then she laughed. Lynn Evans, the perfect modern woman—tough, skeptical, invulnerable, but perfectly happy? Didn't she too want to find the perfect life, the group that would be the perfect family she never had. Hadn't she wanted that with Shirley and ignored all the misery that relationship had brought because she wanted a family so badly?

She said easily then, "It would be wonderful if there was a group that came up with some solutions, some answers for us self-conscious, over-educated, modern mortals. There is a part of me that wants an easier way out—a big mother in the sky who would love and take care of me. Or maybe a community of like-minded people who would understand me, cherish and talk to me, maybe even a few good cooks and companions...I...."

"Something like that is what we're trying to build. Of course I know there is no supernatural in the Western sense of that word. What we believe in is Kali-ma, the She that has many names and many aspects...She is reality, everything."

"Kali-ma, is the name of your leader?"

Marta laughed. "Well, in a manner of speaking, but she's not a person, not one alive today. She's all and none, those who have gone before and those who will come after. She is part of us—and all that is natural. What the Western scientific mind calls nature."

"An old question. If Goddesses exist why aren't things better, especially for women?"

Marta smiled. "That statement presupposes a very simplistic view of reality...of Kali-ma. I think you would be very bored and rebellious in such a world."

"It does intrigue me that your leader is a woman. I'm curious about this person you call the Sister. Is she running the group or is she just a figurehead?"

Marta looked into her tea cup as if she would find the answer there. She finally said without looking up, "The Sister guides us. She is the source of wisdom. Like the Goddess she shows us the path. Hers is not worldly power, the management of organizations and lives."

"In other words, men manage and women guide."

Marta looked up and took Lynn's hands in her own, squeezing them. "I admit the Sister is not a corporate executive. She doesn't send out memos. For some people there is a spiritual realm." She leaned back in her chair laughing.

Suddenly Lynn was overwhelmed. The touch, the sweet sound of her laughter.... There was something about this woman with the velvet skin and magic eyes.... The air between them seemed charged. She heard herself say, "I like reality."

"That brings up the question, what's really real?" Marta's dark eyes sparkled with a teasing humor. "For example, there's something between us; it has light, energy, especially feeling. Your scientists say our bodies and minds operate on electricity. They might name this energy between us electromagnetism or say it is an illusion of the mind of one of us. We in the Society call it sacred and hold it in reverence as an expression, perhaps an aspect of the Goddess Shakti, or Parvati." She released Lynn's hands and placed her fingers lightly on Lynn's face. "...In the same way we hold sacred this flesh that physics says is mere space containing a few clusters of energy they call atoms."

Lynn sipped her tea self-consciously. The energy between them did not lessen. Absorbed in the sound of Marta's voice, Lynn quit listening to the individual words. Even the tiny lines at the corners of Marta's eyes and lips charmed her. Could this be a woman capable of murder? Lynn prided herself on her judgment of people. She could not imagine Marta trying to hurt anyone.

Marta leaned back again and smiled. "I look at your face— blue eyes, a smooth complexion, firm yet delicate bones. There is the sparkle of intelligence in your eye and the curve of your cheekbone hints at Native American in your blood. There is something special about your particular face, and I know that Kali-ma is present. She was with me when I decided to come here with you."

Lynn looked down at the piece of Marta's skirt near her own knee, but saw only her own flushed face reflected many times from the little mirrors sewed into its border. She took a long sip of her tea, letting the sounds of the cafe occupy her mind in order to regain her equilibrium.

Then the energy changed. Even through the hot liquid Lynn could feel it change—was afraid suddenly, absurdly, that Marta had somehow disappeared.

When Lynn looked up, Marta had covered her own face briefly with her hands. Lynn said, "It must make you very tired, talking to skeptics all the time."

"Your personal salvation and an article about us is not why you sought us out today, is it? It's because of Sam."

Lynn was quiet for a moment. "It's true I knew you were a friend of Sam's, but right now I am interested in doing an in-depth article about your group. "

Marta touched Lynn's hand again, a feather brush with the intensity of a bolt of lightning. "I believe you. It's just that the police have already been putting a lot of pressure on us. It's hard enough for us to lose Sam without being accused of his murder."

"Do you believe he was murdered?"

Marta looked out the window. "I suppose it's possible that he fell back into his old ways with drugs, suffered an overdose, and fell and hit his head. It happens." She shook her head. "But he was one of our best successes. Not only had he shaken his habit, but he'd become an integral part of our group working with us to help others. I feel strongly that he wouldn't purposely have killed himself."

"Why would anyone want to kill him?"

She shook her head. "I don't know. He talked about being afraid. I naively assumed he meant afraid of getting back into drugs."

"Did you know he used to sell drugs?"

"What mattered to us, to me, was that he wanted to change—that he had changed."

"Did you know the people he used to hang out with?"

"I saw some of them briefly when they came to his room, but he never let them in."

"Do you have any idea who they might be?"

"No. And that's for the police to find out. We've got enough pain. You must understand; Sam's death will disrupt our work in ways you can't imagine. The trust we had...already we look at each other wondering what we did wrong."

"It's hard to lose somebody you care about."

Marta smiled. "He wasn't a boyfriend—but someone who needed help and some spiritual guidance...and who was learning to help others."

Marta took a deep breath and looked sadly out the window of the cafe. "I dread going back to the house. So crowded. The trouble with cities, besides the expense, is the way you are thrown on top of one another. We're all crammed into a few rooms. Even the most saintly of us wears thin sometimes. If I knew how long we would be here, I would try harder to find my own apartment." She looked up. "Of course it's in the cities that people need most what we can teach. So many people with no center, no presence. I feel sometimes that I'm also losing my self—that it is being sucked away."

"By people like me who have nothing better to do than give you a hard time about what you believe?"

Marta's eyes were a little unfocused now as she turned from the window. She took a sip of tea as if to give herself time to think. Then she said, "No, I wouldn't say that. You know who

21

you are and what you think and feel. You certainly have a center to yourself. It's refreshing—and dangerous."

"Why dangerous?"

"It makes me want...takes me away from my...mission." Marta looked out the window again. "I am aware that you are flirting with me. It threatens to bring back a part of my life...I have been lovers with women too. Now my work is my love...is my life."

She stood up suddenly, gathered her things. "I must be going. It's a long bus ride back to the house and they will be expecting me. A household with so many people requires discipline."

Lynn's head was spinning. As if through a long tunnel, she heard herself say, "You're welcome to stay at my apartment; I have an extra room that has a pull-out couch. It's a very quiet place, on a residential street. My...roommate...my lover left recently." She blushed. "No strings attached."

Marta covered her face with open palms to think it through, then she looked up. It seemed to Lynn that Marta's smile lit up the whole room. "Well, right now, with this police investigation and...just temporarily; it would be a help. I'd repay you some-how." Then she frowned. "You're kind—Lynn, but would it be fair to you? I know you came to talk to me because the police suspect me. I'd have to ask you not to write about the Society while I stay with you. It would be too disruptive if they thought..." She reached in her pocket to find money for the tea. "Thank's very much for the offer, but...."

Lynn shook her head, "I've already mentioned Sam's connection to the Kalimaya Society in yesterday's article, but there's not much that won't appear in other papers anyway. I have no actual assignment at present to cover your group. I came to talk to you on my own for an in-depth article. If my boss asks for it, I'll warn you. So my offer still stands."

Marta closed her eyes and placed her graceful finger tips against the bridge of her nose for a long moment. When she slowly opened her eyes again, her pupils were dilated, her face porcelain smooth, her finger tips touching. "Yes, I'll stay with you a few days. It will give me the respite I need to continue my work. Thank you."

3

Marta directed the taxi driver to a part of town that was still partly residential with tall oaks and a few elms, and where there were still some neighborhood shops among the warehouses and light industry. She told the taxi driver to stop in the middle of a street of tightly packed three story wooden houses, built for working families during the 1880s. The yellow paint of the house they approached was peeling and the tiny front yard was spare, but the broken front stairs were swept clean and there was the smell of fresh spices in the front hall. Lynn waited in the entry way full of coats and bags and boxes of pamphlets while Marta went into one of the rooms and began stuffing things into a big duffel bag.

Lynn could see into an oversized kitchen where people were gathered silently around a large wooden table. Lynn felt she was being dissected by their few glances. The juggler wasn't there. She could see why such a homey place would appeal to someone like Sam, living alone in a seedy hotel with only the desk clerk and Myrtle McCurdy for company. Lynn tried to study the posters and notices on the bulletin board by the front door— meetings in other cities, reports from an ashram in Nepal. She was intrigue by a photo of a rather magnificent Victorian mansion with a label under it in a foreign script.

She turned her back to the kitchen crowd and managed a few stills of the bulletin board with her pocket camera for future reference.

"That's where people like you go to get their heads together."

Lynn turned to look down into a pair of bright blue eyes, peering over a thick sandwich smelling strongly of peanut butter. A small girl, maybe six or seven years old, and dressed in a colorful assortment of slightly oversized clothing, munched slowly. Lynn said rather defensively, "What do you mean, people like me?"

The child swallowed and contemplated the rest of her lumpy whole grain bread. "You know, regular people with tight shoes, grey clothes and too much money."

Lynn was suddenly aware of her feet. They did hurt in their fashionable shoes, but just a little. "Grey is my favorite color. There are lots of shades of gray. This shirt is really blue anyway. Shouldn't you be—doing homework or something?"

"I don't go to school when we're on the road. My mother teaches me. Anyway, travel is educational. Want to see what I painted?"

Lynn glanced toward the kitchen where Marta was talking in a low voice. Lynn managed to smile at the child. "Sure, why not."

The little girl led her into what must have once been the parlor. The worn flower-patterned rug was strewn with pillows and there was an altar in the corner with a brass many-armed female goddess smeared with some sort of white paste and covered with red powder and flower petals. Lit incense sticks in a brass jar gave off a sweet cloying smell.

"She is Kali-ma," the little girl said with authority. She took some papers from a shelf and spread them out. Lynn settled on one of the pillows and studied the drawings. What could one say to a child that didn't sound condescending and insipid? The 'that's nice, dear' kind of words mothers and teachers usually settled on had certainly offended her when she was a budding artist.

Lynn had always thought she didn't like children much. Shirley had said it was because she was afraid to admit she wanted to have them. Some of their worst arguments had been over Shirley's biological clock. Lynn had finally agreed to help take care of a baby should Shirley decide to get inseminated. She had said it to please Shirley, but Shirl hadn't believed her. Domesticity balanced against being a reporter. Lynn hadn't found anything yet that would keep her away from the possibility of a good story. It was easier not to wonder what it would be like to have a kid.

The drawings seemed to be of a series of demons with grinning faces and sharp swords in some of their many hands. The stark red, white, and black paint didn't turn them into cartoon figures. "Mean looking spiders," was her inspired comment.

The child sighed and stood up with fists on hips, a parody of an exasperated mother. "Don't you see it's Kali-ma. She isn't supposed to be goody-goody all the time. She's lots of things. Mother says she is everything. She's fierce sometimes, especially when her friends are in trouble. Mother says people call her a mean demon goddess because they are afraid of her power."

Out of the mouths of babes. Lynn wondered if this kid really wanted to tell her something or just wanted her paintings admired. "Are her friends in trouble? It's hard when your friends are in trouble. It's sad that Sam died."

"Sam wasn't *my* friend. Anyway, people are always in trouble, dummy. You're a grown-up. You ought to know that. Mother says we can't always understand the wisdom of the goddess."

"Didn't your mother teach you not to call grown-ups dummy?"

The child said sulkily, "You must be a dummy or else you'd know better'n to take Marta away from us when she's on a mission. Everybody'll be pissed. She shouldn't have brought you here. You're lucky Jason isn't here to stop you. He says people like you are only supposed to come to meetings and give us money."

Someone called from the kitchen and the girl disappeared through the door. Lynn could hear tense low voices as if on the verge of an argument. She followed the child.

The room became deadly silent when Lynn came in. The little girl clung to a woman Marta was arguing with. She said into the woman's dress in a whiny voice that echoed in the silent room, "Why can't she just stay here too, Nancy? Marta's bed is big enough."

Marta flushed and said, "This is Lynn Evans. She has kindly offered me a room for a few days." Nancy just glared at her and the others at the table did not look at Lynn. Marta went to the table and took some money out of a drawer, saying, "I'll take one week's share now and I'll talk to the Sister myself."

Nancy said to the little girl, her resentment showing in her voice. "She's getting too important to share our space. Just like

25

Jason, the Sister's pet." She said to Marta, her voice petulant, "I didn't think you would desert us so soon."

Marta sighed and sat down at the table. "Nancy, I'm not leaving the work. I'll be with you every day. It's just that this kind woman has offered me a place to stay temporarily—a quiet space with some privacy."

Nancy glared at Lynn, eyelids lowered in anger. "I know what you want that privacy for."

A younger woman looked up from her cup of tea and said quietly, "You know what the Sister would say about that kind of remark, Nancy."

Nancy ignored her and said, as if speaking for the group, "The Sister will be very angry with you for leaving us now."

Marta didn't move. She looked down at the money in her hand as if questioning her decision. But then she said, "I'm not a personal servant to Kali-ma. Our way gives me freedom of choice as well as responsibility. I need some time for myself so that I can do the work the Society asks of me."

Nancy stepped closer to Marta. "Not choice over responsibility."

There was an ominous silence in the room. Lynn shouldered the duffel bag and said as calmly as she could, "There's a taxi waiting. We'd better go."

Nancy stepped between Lynn and Marta as if to interfere. The young woman who had confronted Nancy pulled Marta into a seat next to her at the table and whispered something in her ear. Marta reached out and the group at the table began clasping each others hands. Nancy picked up her cup of tea and left the room unceremoniously with the little girl following reluctantly.

They sat still and silent for what seemed, to Lynn, an interminable time. She wanted to grab Marta and pull her from the chair. Instead she stepped closer and touched her arm. Marta got up quickly and went around the table giving each one a hug and a whispered word. Then she followed Lynn out the door.

Once in the taxi, Marta said breathlessly, "It'll be OK. They aren't used to managing on their own, but they'll soon be glad for the extra room."

Lynn was puzzled. "Would they have tried to make you stay?"

Marta didn't look at Lynn as she nervously smoothed out her

skirt and shifted her duffel. Her speech was hesitant, careful, as if she were sifting through words for the right ones. "There is some...controversy in our...leadership at the moment. Sometimes it's...difficult. But you shouldn't judge the whole of our philosophy, our teachings, by the behavior of some individuals. I try not to get caught up in it, but to keep a clear vision. Leaving right now will help me do that."

Lynn unlocked the door to her loft apartment, remembering only after she switched on the light that the place was a mess. She was embarrassed at the disarray. It hadn't seemed so terrible when she had left that morning. But now the clothesline, stretched across the middle of the room, with her newly-printed photographs hanging on it looked tacky, to say the least. There were books, papers and clothes everywhere. She had sacrificed her kitchen sink to the photo process and the room smelled of chemicals.

She opened a window and tried hurriedly to straighten up some of the clutter. Now that Shirley was gone, the loft showed her own lack of order. In spite of the loneliness these last few weeks, Lynn had been relieved at the absence of Shirley's organizing impulses. Now things were where Lynn had left them and easy to find.

By the time Lynn was ready to sit down with a beer, Marta had put her duffel in the spare room, cleaned up the kitchen corner of the loft, unloaded the bags of groceries Lynn had bought, and was already cooking...and Lynn was madly in love.

Dinner consisted of fruit curry and rice, tea and a delicious unleavened bread. Lynn had found some Eastern music to play; Shirl had not taken all the tapes.

As she sat, barely able to sip her tea, the skeptical Lynn, the one who wanted to write a tough but insightful article about the Kalimaya Society, muttered helplessly about getting involved with murder suspects and about how she hated tea without milk or honey.

Still she waited self-consciously for Marta's brown eyes to swallow her again, for that voice to drown her.

Marta got up, gathering the dishes swiftly and began washing them. Lynn sat helplessly trying to think of something to say. Then Marta disappeared into Shirl's study.

A few minutes later she reappeared, dressed to go out. "I'll be late. Do you have an extra key so I won't have to wake you?"

Lynn went to the drawer in her desk where Shirl had left her good-bye note and her key. She silently handed it to Marta. The coral lips smiled gently. "Thank you."

The loft seemed terribly empty after Marta was gone. Somehow all the urgent projects Lynn had been so frantically trying to finish this week didn't seem so important any more.

She couldn't even force herself to print any blow-ups of the murder scene. After all, she didn't want grisly pictures hanging over the sink when Marta came back. Instead, she took out her magnifying glass to look at the contact sheet.

She was jolted out of her euphoria when she spotted someone who looked like the juggler, Jason, in one of the crowd shots. She didn't like that man. He certainly hadn't spent all afternoon handing out pamphlets in the park. She would have to show this to Del.

Lynn was lying awake around two a.m. in the dark when the door opened quietly. She listened anxiously as Marta prepared for bed. They had not even discussed where Marta would sleep. Would she pull out the couch in Shirl's room where there was a quilt? Would she drag her sleeping bag out of the big duffel? Lynn had planned to offer part of her own queen-sized water bed, assuming there would be a long evening after dinner in which a conversation on the subject would take place. The sensible Lynn sneered at herself—pull yourself together, girl. Can't let a little flirtation get in the way of a story—things are complicated enough already—no seductions please. But when she finally fell asleep, she dreamed of brown eyes and silky skin.

• • •

Lynn got up quietly the next morning to go to work. Marta was curled up in her sleeping bag on the couch in the spare room and didn't wake up.

In the afternoon Lynn went back to the Emery Hotel to interview the desk clerk, Nelson, who had been there at the time of the murder. But she learned no more than she already knew from Del and Detective Thomas.

Standing next to her at the desk was an older, gray-haired

man sorting his mail. He snapped, "You see God punishes those who flaunt His commandments." He threw an advertisement aggressively into the overflowing waste basket next to the desk. Without another word, he took two thin letters and moved toward the staircase. Lynn followed him. "Did you know Sam Jenson?"

"I know what he was."

"And what was that?"

"Who are you?"

She handed him her card. Standing stiffly at the base of the stairs, he read it and gave it back. "He was one of those tempted by Satan and Satan's minions." The man's voice had the resonance of someone trained for the pulpit.

Lynn held out her hand. "Reverend...?"

"Mister Arthur J. Collins. I don't hold with titles. Another temptation of the Devil."

Lynn wanted to ask what he did hold with, but she also wanted to avoid a sermon if possible. "Will you tell me what you know about the deceased?"

He gave her a long look with penetrating glass-green eyes. "Come upstairs. I want my tea; I've had a long day."

His room, across from Sam's, was very neat. Religious pamphlets were arranged on the only table so that the titles could be read. A small bookshelf held thick books, well dusted, from Thomas Aquinas to Mary Baker Eddy.

She got out her tape recorder and set it on the table, but did not turn it on. Mr. Collins got out two china cups and saucers and put them on a TV tray already laid out with napkins and a sugar bowl. He poured her a cup of tea with the milk already in it from a red plastic thermos. It was not quite hot, but she sipped it anyway.

On the dresser next to a very clean comb and brush set there was a picture of a handsome woman holding a baby.

"Your wife and child?"

He looked over at the picture with a studied disinterest, but she could see that his hands were shaking. "My wife left long ago. Good riddance to her too. No, that is my mother."

"And you?"

He nodded. "She passed away." His face reddened slightly

and he looked away. "Thieves, Devil-possessed...no doubt drug addicts too. They attacked her. She was nearly eighty...had a heart attack." His lips trembled. "They got nothing. Her death for nothing."

"I'm very sorry." Lynn waited a moment. "Where do you work, Mr. Collins?"

He spread a napkin across his lap and opened a box of crackers from the drawer in the table. "I earn money as an accountant...independent.... I keep my own hours. It leaves me time for my real work. My wife didn't approve; not enough money for her indulgences. Another Devil worshiper, I'm afraid. Are you going to turn that thing on? If you are doing a piece on me, there are some things I would like to say."

She obliged him and he began what could only be described as a sermon on the Devil as cause of all worldly ills, but one that did not quite make sense.

When he paused to take a sip of tea she said, "Tell me about Sam."

"I already gave a statement to the police."

"I don't have access to that. My readers will be interested in what you know."

He got up rather abruptly, walked to the window and pointed toward a small city park. "See there." Lynn went to the window. She could see the edge of a tiny crowd. Juggling balls appeared above their heads. As she watched, the little girl she had talked to the day before appeared with a basket to collect money.

"It's that devil cult Sam was part of. I've been keeping track of them. Sam Jenson is dead and yet they are still coming here to spread their evil lies."

"I've heard they got him off drugs."

Mr. Collins sat down again, suddenly calm. He poured himself more tea. His eyes were wide, his pupils dilated. It was as if another person were speaking as he said softly, "They are everywhere. That particular bunch of blunderers is nothing. They will bring about their own perdition." He smiled slightly. "You know there are a myriad of ways; Evil is hidden behind the purest face, always waiting underneath each entrapping smile."

"Who do you mean?"

He leaned closer. "We will stop them because they can not

avoid showing us their true natures."

"Who?"

His voice boomed again. "All those who have denied God's word." He picked up some pamphlets. His hands were shaking again. She felt a little frightened of him.

He changed again as suddenly. "You will print...what I said?" His voice had a begging quality now.

"Well, I intended to research Sam's death."

"He was no-good, unsavable. Why write about him? Newspapers are full of evil-doings. Satan invented the media to seduce us into evil."

"So you weren't on friendly terms with Sam?"

"He ended any possible friendly terms with me when he joined them. He knew very well I didn't approve. In the beginning he listened to me. I got him to question...his ways. Then they came and turned him from the true path. He became one of them—evil—arrogant in his ignorance."

"Did you talk to him lately? Did he seem depressed or?—"

Arthur Collin's voice was angry now. "He had the joy on him of the wicked. He flaunted his contempt for my truths." He leaned forward conspiratorially. The glint in his eyes was almost frightening. "I saw the Devil visit him."

Lynn leaned forward. "Tell me about it."

"In the form of a woman—dark with slanted eyes. I heard it first from behind me. Ornaments that rattled and flashed in the hall light. I watched it go into his room." Arthur Collins was a different man now. Before his movements had been abrupt, controlled and almost stiff. Now his gestures were fluid, almost sensuous, as his fingers drew images in the air between them. "Another Devil yesterday. Thin, almost black... He left sweet smelling smoke in the hallway, a sure sign...had on a white suit, but it didn't fool me."

Lynn's news radar kicked in. Arthur had possibly seen Sam's killer. "What time of day did 'white suit' visit Sam?"

Arthur pulled out a gold pocket watch as if to orient himself. "I was coming home for lunch. It had to be four o'clock when I last saw her—day before yesterday." He next consulted the small calendar in his wallet and then the one on the wall above the table. He had made copious notes on it, though Lynn was not close enough to read the neat, tiny writing.

The controlled tone came back into his voice. "I had just gone down to put out the garbage when I noticed a sulphur smell then saw...that thing in the white suit. I always take my garbage out exactly at twelve-thirty." He pursed his lips. "They still haven't collected it. Sometimes it's a whole week before they collect it." He shuddered slightly.

Lynn thought, you smelled rotting garbage. But she said, "The elevator was working?"

"As much as I hate the filth of the back stairs I never use the elevator. One could get trapped in that iron cage; the cables are so old."

Del had told Lynn that the time of Jenson's death was about one o'clock. "Did you tell the police about this man you saw?"

Arthur looked at her strangely. Then he put down his tea cup and carefully closed the lid of his thermos. "As I said, the Devil comes in many guises. One must speak of Him with caution to those in authority. I told them what I saw but let them believe it was a person."

This guy was crazy, but enough to have killed Sam? Was he inventing the devil in a white suit story because, as he had said, he was mad at Sam for not listening to him anymore? She got up, moving closer to the door before he could once again launch into his sermonizing speech. She thanked him for the tea, took a couple of photos, made some reassuring but non-committal remarks about including him in an article and left.

When she got home that evening there was a lingering fragrance. It took Lynn a few moments to recognize it—the same incense had been burning at the group's house. A plate of food had been left covered on the table. The only reassurance that Marta would return was her bundle of belongings in the closet of the spare room, yet the whole apartment seemed filled with her presence.

4

First thing next morning when she arrived at her office in the Chronicle building, Lynn made a phone call to Del Whitney. As usual she offered some information expecting information she wanted in return.

"She's staying with you?" Del asked after Lynn told her about her meeting with Marta. "Rog'll have a conniption. Even I think that's a bit far to go for a story."

Annoyed, Lynn said, "I didn't arrange it that way; it just happened. She needed a temporary retreat. If you had seen the tension in that house...."

"Yeh sure.... Just keep us posted. I can tell by the sound of your voice that you're sure she's innocent. I've heard of co-opting the press, but this takes the cake."

Del chuckled, but Lynn bristled. "I thought it was a good opportunity."

Del laughed again.

"Stop it."

"Just the facts, ma'am."

Lynn felt her face flushing and was glad Del couldn't see her. "You want my cooperation, you better be nice to me."

"OK, OK, we're not sure she's involved anyway."

"Any new information?"

"Keep it under your hat for now, but a couple of guys off the street who knew Sam before he got religion don't have alibis. They're small time though—petty pushers. No sign of your dude in cowboy boots. If our bum wasn't so nervous about the whole thing, I'd think it was all made up."

"Mr. Bailey. His name is Mr. Bailey."

Del snickered.

"What's so funny?"

"Her name is *Ms* Bailey, Lou Ellen Bailey. She says it's safer if people think she's a man. Fewer hassles. She works at it."

"A bag lady in drag?" Lynn shook her head and stared at people passing in the street below.

"Unfortunately she was out cold except when Cowboy Boots tromped over her."

"Tromped over her?"

"That's what she says. She does have some bruises."

"You think he could be the murderer?"

Del was getting impatient. "Lou Ellen didn't get his fingerprints."

"What about the piece of metal from the broken elevator?"

"We found it in the trash. Could be the cause of the blow to the head, but there weren't any fingerprints on it, and the coroner says the blow didn't kill Jenson anyway. It was a combination of drugs and alcohol. We found a whiskey bottle in the closet; no prints on that either."

"I talked to Mr. Arthur Collins, the ultra-Christian neighbor. I'll get you a copy of my interview."

"He's certifiable. Can't tell what he saw and what he made up."

"He saw a dark guy in a white suit go into Sam's apartment about noon."

Del snorted. "You mean the Devil."

"Could it have been someone in the Kalimaya Society?"

"We're checking it out. He didn't tell us about the white suit." There was a pause then Del said, "What did you find out from your house guest?"

"Not much. Sam was one of their successes. She is hard to figure out. Talks a lot but doesn't say much, at least nothing personal. I don't know where she goes. Her people hang out at the parks recruiting. I haven't checked out the downtown office yet."

Del heard the disappointment Lynn couldn't keep out of her voice and said sympathetically, "Well, keep an eye on her, but don't get too romantic yet. I don't think you're into long-distance relationships, and this lady may be spending some time away."

Lynn didn't answer, so Del said, "You will tell us if you find out anything we need to know?"

"Thanks for the vote of confidence Del."

Del sighed. "Bye now, hon."

Lynn said good-bye. Sometimes Del could be such a pain.

Lynn's end of the office she shared on the second floor at the *Chronicle,* unlike her apartment, was neat, with only a filing cabinet next to an uncluttered desk with its telephone and computer terminal. She sat staring through the only window at the few scraggly trees struggling to survive in a sea of concrete and asphalt in front of the old red brick City Hall building across the street. Then she turned on her computer to begin writing up her notes on Mr. Collins.

"Fresh pot, come and get it." The voice belonged to her officemate, Bill Fuller, now filling the doorway with his bulk, coffee cup in hand, tie perpetually loosened. He took one long stride and sat down in his swivel chair, feet up on the desk.

Lynn said, not breaking the flow of typing and ignoring the fact that he had not offered to get her a cup, "No thanks, just got here."

Bill set down his cup carefully on the large and randomly placed pile of papers on his desk and said, "I don't know how you do that."

She stopped, annoyed because he had managed to distract her and turned from her computer. She contemplated the other half of the window that was filled with a healthy green clutter of plants belonging to Bill. It matched his half of the office with its organized pile of paper and books, the walls full of photos surrounding a giant map of the city. "What?"

"Type and talk at the same time."

"I can use both sides of my brain."

"Is that a slam at male-type, linear thinking?"

"If the shoe fits...."

Now that he had her attention he said, "Boss wants to see you in her office." He sat back and sipped at his coffee. When she got up he asked casually, "What's up?"

"No doubt it's about my last article. Not enough on the Kalimaya Society and its connection to Sam Jenson's death."

"Gale is not one to worry about getting sued, so, like I said, what's up?"

"It probably wasn't tough enough. I want to stay on the Society's good side so I can get an interview with the guru."

Bill shrugged. "Sounds good to me."

Lynn suspected if her boss Gale Donahue had been born a male, she'd be one that smoked cigars, was balding and a bit vain about his looks. As it was, she was what Lynn's mother would have called sturdy and a little crass. But Gale's manner was a thin cover for her journalistic genius and remarkable facility for detecting and recycling bullshit.

When Lynn walked into the chief editor's office, Gale was weighing her article in one fist. "What is this stuff? Not even an interview with the main guru? A member of the Kalimayas is murdered and you interview a lady who cleaned his apartment. Come on, do you need a vacation—maybe a long vacation? Where did this cult get the money to start their retreat in the Himalayas? What is their leadership like? I want you to follow up on them. And none of this namby-pamby stuff. Where is my cynical investigative reporter? Do I have to put you back on movie reviews? I would think this cult stuff would be right up your alley. A real drop back into patriarchal Dark Ages. Or are you going soft in your old age?"

Lynn felt her guts twist. Her cynical side warned, Now it's on the line girl. Put up or shut up. The part of her that was newly in love writhed in doubt; if she wrote the article Gale wanted, she would never see Marta again.

When Lynn didn't answer, Gale sat down on her desk. "What is going on? I know that Shirley's leaving was hard on you but...."

"Look, I have an in with the detectives in charge of the investigation. I figured I would get more from them if I took it easy on the speculation until there was more conclusive evidence. Anyway, if I start out hard line on these Kalimayas, I'll never get close enough for a decent interview. In fact, a woman, one of their leaders, Marta Handley is staying with me for a few days— needs some time out from the group. She's my link with the cult. I want to find out what she knows."

Gale leaned back in her chair and nodded. "Not a bad idea. Get more from the inside of this thing. You do have an instinct for a good story. Be careful though; try not to get too... involved...especially if she's a suspect in Jenson's death." Gale gave her a peck on the cheek. Lynn hated the condescension in the gesture. Gale had a habit of treating emotional life as if it were an illness—the insight of a woman and the attitude of a man. But Lynn was relieved to be off the hook for a while.

She spent the next few hours researching the Kalimaya Society. It was estimated that, in this city alone, they already had a thousand followers. She found a few brief articles about parents who wanted their teenagers to leave the cult. The articles followed the group's activities across the U.S: meetings, interviews in different cities, a drug arrest of an ex-member, accounts of members being evicted, threats of civil suits, innuendoes about consorting with the Devil. One member filed a discrimination suit against her company after being fired for having an altar in her office and burning incense. A rather dry Sunday supplement article discussed the influence of various Eastern philosophies on the Kalimayas indicating that the leaders have an understanding of classical Hindu religion and the place of Buddhist thought.

Strangely, none of the articles had actual quotes from the Society's guru, a woman called simply The Sister. One article had a picture of a public meeting with a fuzzy photo of the guru held by several followers. Was one of them the juggler she had seen with Marta?

Gale had given Lynn an article from the *Hastings Weekly*, a small suburban paper. There was a large red arrow and a note, *See page three*. There, in a long article, *Cult Members Worship Goddess*, Lynn read:

Our fair city has been graced with the presence of a new Fad. It involves a cult that incorporates in its message a wide selection of Eastern religious beliefs. Central to it, however, is the worship of Kali, the rather bloodthirsty goddess popular in India.

The cult's message is powerful enough to have had a marked effect on the fashions of several of the local high schools. Indian silk and cotton prints, jewelry, pierced noses and ears, as well as a few shaved heads have appeared. Some of our more solid citizens have been known to frequent a recently acquired retreat somewhere in the woods of the northern part of the state. This reporter is amazed that the jars they carry around on their forays soliciting in the streets could accumulate enough cash for the down payment on such an estate.

When this reporter attempted to interview some of the leadership of this Kali worshiping cult, he was told that, "Our Sister does not believe in interviews as a method of disseminating truth." What are they hiding?

She was suddenly very curious about this woman referred to simply as The Sister. A woman as guru. Marta had mentioned her. Why hadn't anyone been able to interview her? Where was she? An interview with a woman cult leader was definitely worth some effort.

Lynn threw down the newspaper. It was time to get some answers.

She called the number on the card that Marta had given her. A man with an East Indian accent answered. Collins' description of the Devil in a white suit crossed Lynn's mind. She asked for an interview with the guru mentioned by both the suburban rag and Marta as The Sister.

"Our Sister is in retreat and generally does not give interviews. However, you may have an opportunity to see her at a public meeting this afternoon." He gave the address—an old opera house turned movie theater in a seedy part of town.

• • •

The old theater was nestled among shabby Victorian buildings, warehouses, pawnbrokers and used furniture dealers. Outside the theater, behind dusty glass, the edges of gaudy torn pictures of movie stars peaked out from beneath a freshly printed poster of the many-armed Goddess. The Goddess looked at Lynn with a disturbingly modern face, her many hands carrying the tools of modern technology rather than ancient weapons. A single eye in the center of her forehead stared at Lynn questioningly making her wonder why she was here. In the past she had avoided cults. They made her uncomfortable—too close to the edge of sanity perhaps.

The lobby showed more caring preparation than the outside of the theater. Fresh flowers and draped fabrics on newly painted walls, made the faded grandeur of the the place come alive.

The crowd was a strange mixture—teenagers in T-shirts,

suburban housewives, leather-clad motorcyclists and gray-haired businessmen. Lynn spotted Marta looking wonderful in a peacock blue sari among the clusters of people already gathered inside the lobby. Lynn pushed her way through the people to reach Marta as the crowd moved into the theater itself.

A small group of Kalimayas stood in front of the stage—the men in formal white suits, the women in bright silk saris. Marta joined this group before Lynn could catch up with her. Lynn recognized the juggler, Jason, in a white suit that was a bit too small for his bulky frame. He looked uncomfortable and stiff.

On the stage an altar held a huge offering of fresh flowers. The living flowers seemed to glow against the surroundings of dusty theater props. Lynn looked over the audience. Some of the people from the house were there. The woman, Nancy, who had given Marta such a hard time recognized her and, frowning, turned away.

Lynn moved closer to the group near the stage to listen. A diminutive dark woman in a red sari was talking in an animated almost musical voice. "Tonight you, not as separate individuals, but as a tiny, missing fragment of the Goddess, will rejoin her essence. We will touch and be one again."

As Lynn moved forward, Jason noticed her and leaned seductively toward Marta to whisper something.

Marta looked into Lynn's eyes seeming to read her thoughts. "I hope you will look past your reporter nose tonight. I will introduced you to the Sister and then perhaps you will understand."

Had the woman in the red sari heard Marta? In any case she turned toward Lynn and unexpectedly took her hands. At her shoulder Marta said, "Lynn Evans, this is our Sister."

The Sister's eyes held a terrifying depth, different from the comfort of Marta's warm brown ones. "Marta has spoken of you. Thank you for your kindness. The last few days have been a trial to our little sister."

Lynn was flustered at the genuine gratitude in her voice, and, unable to respond in kind, merely mumbled, "Pleased to meet you," while starting to back away to a safer distance. Then her reporter self kicked in and she said, "Can you tell me a little about yourself and the history of this Society. It's so unusual to find a woman—"

A tall, lean man interrupted, moving rather roughly between Lynn and the Sister and grabbed Lynn's arm to lead her away. Annoyed, she looked up into his stiff but smiling face as she pulled away. He said, "We are about to start. My name is Singh, Mr. Rajid Singh. If you come to me after the meeting, we can set up an appointment to answer your questions."

"With the Sister?"

"I am sorry. That will be impossible."

Lynn turned back to speak with Marta and the Sister again, but they were already on their way onto the stage. The lights dimmed and Lynn was forced to find a seat.

Pushing a candy wrapper off the worn red velvet, she took a seat near the front. The smell of mildew and stale popcorn reminded her of the time her grandmother had taken her to a vaudeville show and movie in just such a theater. Then it had been magical. Now.... What she would give for a fresh bag of popcorn. A man sat down in the empty seat next to her. She was relieved to see he had a press badge, though she couldn't quite read the paper's name written on it.

She looked at his face in the dim light. Finally she recognized Peter O'Hara, a reporter from her paper's rival newspaper, *The Hartfield Times*. He returned her glance with an amused smile. Did he think she was a Kalimaya convert?

Brass bells and gongs cleared the air and the audience quieted. Onstage, the bowl of flowers now glowed as if with an internal light. Lynn leaned toward Peter and whispered, "An electric light under the glass bowl, no doubt. Very effective don't you think?" Peter gave a slight nod and a smile of amusement.

Women dressed in voluminous saris walked slowly down the aisles swinging incense pots before them, then lit candles all over the theater. "Has to be against the fire rules," she whispered to Peter and she felt a disapproving rustle of motion around her. Now she wished she had sat in the back so she could watch or leave without bothering anybody.

Quiet chanting began, enough to lull her to sleep. Lynn leaned back, dreaming of fire and of glass melting to make something beautiful. The transparent body of a woman formed, then melted and then formed again—pure light. Lynn's eyes opened suddenly to stare into a terrifying huge single eye that blinked slowly in the dark.

On the stage the pulsing light that had been hidden under the flowers, now streamed from a huge blinking eye, a cheap conjurer's trick, not even worthy of a vaudeville act. Lynn turned to her neighbor. His face was placid, even amused. Was he laughing at her for being startled?

Her reporter self surfaced like a determined swimmer after being thrown by a tidal wave. What angle could she use? How was she going to get past the Sister's vigilant body guard? She'd have to grab Peter later and exchange notes—find out if he knew anything important. And make it clear to him she wasn't attached to this group.

The pulsing light was giving her a headache, or was it the incense? Lynn's face suddenly felt hot, her forehead tingled. On stage the eye formed a red light which opened slowly into undulating petal shapes and she felt that her mind would burst open. She almost laughed at the image; her mind bursting open like a flower. Then the eye reappeared but now it was larger and in the iris the blossom still opened.

She could not get rid of the phony eye image even after it faded. It was still there when she closed her lids. It attracted and fascinated her even as she felt invaded and exposed...and terrified She was about to brave the aisles for a quick exit, when, mercifully, bells were played again and more candles were lit.

One by one women from the audience went forward with a candle and knelt in front of the altar of flowers. Soon the air was again filled with the soft seductive sound of women's voices chanting. Lynn felt a strong urge to join them in conflict with her urge to escape. Then out of the corner of her eye she thought she saw Marta coming toward her from the side of the stage and beckoning to her. She sat frozen with fear as if an abyss of insanity lay at the edge of the stage.

Then the critical voice inside chided her not to take these feelings so seriously; as a reporter she should think nothing of joining in this ritual if she could get more information.

She forced herself to follow the women as they formed a large circle of candlelight around the altar. When Marta took her hand a joyful bubble of laughter replaced the terror, sneaking up into her chest, though she didn't know what the joke was.

Hold on girl, you're slipping, came from somewhere in the back of her mind, but she still found herself laughing. Marta's soft hand took her arm and led her to the altar. She felt a cool drop of water on the center of her forehead. The Sister took something sweet-smelling from a little bowl and touched it to her temples. Then she took Lynn's hands and dipped her fingers in the bowl of flowers and touched them to her own forehead. This time there was a question in her eyes, an invading question that searched through Lynn's mind—a frightening question: Who are you, really—the deepest sense of you?

Lynn suddenly felt swallowed up by the light, the incense, the flowers at the altar. No, she did not want to be a separate person alone in the cold vastness but...she felt a terribly deep fear. Was she coming to pieces? Melting into...?

Again the voice at the back of her mind came to the rescue. *Scared of a little rice water and mumbo jumbo, kid? You're hallucinating. They put something in the incense. Your cousins got you once when you were ten with their ghost-voodoo stories. You gonna let this little lady get you?*

She glanced back at the audience and saw the shadow of a smile on Peter's face. She felt hot. Suddenly she couldn't breathe; she had to get out. She pulled away from the circle and hurried up the aisle in the dark. Then she was outside under the merciful yellow street light.

She went into the bar across the street and ordered a beer. What a relief to talk to regular people! But she couldn't get Marta out of her mind.

After a while she turned away from the noisy television and went to the door of the bar to see if anyone was coming out of the theater. Maybe she should have stayed; maybe she should go back. Peter O'Hara came out of the theater and she motioned for him to come over, introducing herself again, explaining rather too profusely that she was not a member of the cult while he ordered a drink.

As Peter blew the foam off his beer he asked, "Got an angle for an article?"

Lynn laughed and shrugged. "How about *Woman Guru Sways Vast Crowds*, or *Kinky Sari Newest Fashion in Cult*

Wear." She shook her head and took another swallow of beer. "My editor thinks the religious stuff might be a fake." She didn't mention Sam Jenson's murder. Most papers had treated it as a suicide and had given it little coverage.

Peter said, "I've been following these Kali worshipers off and on since they've been in this part of the country. There is nothing concrete. Lots of innuendo—rumor. Their growth rate is quite impressive. They even seem to be doing some people some good. Especially them that has the cash to pay for the Society's particular brand of psycho-spiritual therapy."

"You think they're worth further investigation, maybe an exposé?" Lynn asked.

He took a swig of his beer and smiled. "Good luck on an exposé." He shook his head. "You'll need to appear at least sympathetic to their cause. I, personally, could never keep a straight face. But if you have any luck, how about sharing what you find out? I'll let you in on some of my leads; you can take a look at my files."

Lynn realized he thought she was trying to look like a convert in order to get a story. She decided not to indicate anything different, not yet anyway. "What ya got?"

Peter settled down on a bar stool. "Lots of their converts are ex-druggies, even some ex-pushers. Like that guy, Sam whats-his-face, who killed himself...or was killed. They have connections in Asia, you know, ashrams and all. One has to wonder how they are really financed. You got a clue? Seen anything suspicious? I saw your article. Not up to your usual. What are you holding back?"

Lynn wasn't about to admit how little she did know. "They collect money on the street."

Peter laughed. "Pennies in buckets didn't build a retreat in Nepal. Frankly I think this thing might be a cover for drug running."

"Any evidence?"

"If there was any hard evidence, the police would be on them." He stood up and stretched. "Call me if you find out anything. We can work on it together. It could be big."

After Peter left, Lynn went back to the theater, first picking up a small camera that she always kept in her car. She wasn't sure now what she had in mind. She had to understand more. There was nothing like good photos to put things in perspective and show that all the things happening in that theater were real, not magical or supernatural.

Back inside, a ritual was taking place on the stage. A red liquid—could it be blood?—was being poured on a black eight-armed Kali statue with a necklace of skulls. Lynn moved down the outside aisle as quietly as she could. She braced herself against the wall for stability to get decent time exposures with her fast film. This was certainly no place for a flash.

Then she noticed a woman watching her. She glanced away and when she looked again, she saw something strange in the middle of the woman's forehead. It looked like an eye and it blinked at her, then it closed and disappeared. Her imagination was getting the better of her. She took a picture and the woman turned anxiously away.

Now she saw Marta alone on the stage. Lynn took more pictures as Marta made a few announcements including a schedule of meetings. The women in saris went around the room with bowls and baskets to collect money. Then the Sister came back on stage, but she did not speak. She began to walk down the aisles handing out flowers and was soon surrounded by followers. Maybe this was the chance to question this elusive woman.

Lynn pushed into the crowd around the Sister to listen to what she was saying.

"Symbols have great power. Worldly symbols—a McDonald's sign—have great power. They touch the inner mind. One can be lost to such symbols. Here, in the technological world of object worship, we must overcome much to reach the inner resources of the mind, to teach it to know itself."

Someone asked, "Why is everything so symbolic? I'm confused by all the images, the symbols. Is there something I can read to explain all the visual elements?"

The Sister smiled. "Let the mind learn in another way. The symbols will become clear with time as you open yourself and go beyond illusion."

Marta appeared quietly to whisk the Sister away. Lynn couldn't get closer through the crowd. She tried to catch Marta's eye. Was she deliberately not noticing?

Left in her wake, Mr. Singh smiled condescendingly, speaking as if to children. "Everything is illusion but Kali-ma." There was a long pause while the crowd grew silent again. He continued, "The Goddess is not in a piece of paper, a book or in a painting, but one can contemplate a painting to feel her presence. Through such symbols we cut through the illusion to touch the powerful center of the self, what Western psychiatry calls the Unconscious."

Lynn resisted the impulse to follow Marta and instead put on her best eye-batting, smooth-cheeked innocent look in hopes of disarming Mr. Singh. By the time she left the theater she had an appointment with him to discuss her 'confusions'.

Marta was not home when Lynn got back to the loft. Nor did she come home that night.

The next day at work, Lynn worried about what had happened at the theater. Was Marta angry? Did she know that Lynn had taken photos? Lynn developed the negatives at work, but saved the printing to do at home. If there was something illegal going on...Lynn could feel the seeds of doubt sprouting and growing like crab grass, choking her image of Marta. Did she want to prove to Marta that her organization was not what it seemed? Or was it Marta who was not what she seemed? Maybe it was better not to know, not to see the rot in the curtains, better to see the phony flowers as real.

She needed to talk to someone so she called Del. "How about I grab a pizza and meet you around six."

"Grab some steaks and veggies, maybe a pie and you're on. Can you pick up the kid on your way?"

Lynn laughed. She liked to play Dad to Del's son, Danny. It was fun to spend time with kids occasionally, especially when they were already big enough so they could talk and occasionally laugh at stupid jokes. And they could be handed back to Mommy. She would have done it more often except that sometimes she ran into a boyfriend of Del's or, worse, some of the teenage friends of Del's daughter Alita.

She stopped by the school playground and picked up the eight-year-old from the basketball court. Once in the car Danny looked in the grocery bag and grabbed some cookies—Lynn had gotten his favorite fruit bars. They talked about basketball and school on the drive home.

At Del's apartment Lynn let herself in with Danny's key. He instantly plunked himself in front of the TV. Alita wasn't home. Lynn washed the breakfast dishes and put on some rice to cook. She was making the salad when Del walked in, dropped her briefcase in the corner, opened a beer and gave Lynn a hug before collapsing into a chair.

Lynn said, "What I won't do for a story."

Del laughed. "Hon, you love it. Satisfies your mothering instinct and reassures you that you really don't want to have kids." Del sat enjoying her beer, then asked, "Alita in her room?"

"Haven't seen her."

Del went to look. When she came back she went to the phone muttering, "Damn it, it's after six o'clock; she should be here doing her homework."

While Lynn put on the steaks, Del called around, finally locating Alita at a friend's house. "You're supposed to leave me a note or call.... Right now...because I say."

"I could pick her up," Lynn offered. Del waved her away impatiently. She hung up the phone and started to set the table.

Half way through dinner Alita stormed into the house and toward her room. Del called, "Are you going to eat?"

A loud "No," was her daughter's response. Del sighed and said, "I don't know why we bother buying her food."

"Don't talk about me as if I'm not here." Alita yelled still out of sight.

Del and Lynn exchanged glances. "She and Ms. Lou Ellen Bailey must have gotten together to take a stand against us oppressive types," Del teased. The door to Alita's room slammed shut.

"Was Bailey any help?" Lynn asked.

Del shrugged. "She didn't identify anyone if that's what you mean. I think she knows more about the neighborhood goings on than she's telling us. I'm keeping an eye on her."

After dinner Del sat on the couch and Danny crawled into her lap. Lynn thought how lovely to be able to do that. Why couldn't there be a giant goddess with an ample soft lap that one could curl up in? Her own mother had been rather cold—didn't like to be touched. Of course, she always gave the obligatory peck on the cheek. She was skinnier than Lynn and just got thinner as she got older, finally turning tough and leathery.

Lynn's parents had run a real estate business and had always been on the go. In the evenings when she was a teenager her parents were often gone—her father to the Rotary or the Lions Club, her mother out to play bridge or to show a house. Dinners at home had been tasteless but adequate. Because her parents were in business together, they didn't talk at home except about problems at work. Her father said conversation at the dinner table gave him indigestion. Now she realized that her father's tension and the struggle to keep her two sisters from fighting had prevented her mother from eating. Her father's tension that finally ended in his early heart attack.

It had sometimes seemed to Lynn as if everyone in her family saw her only as a nuisance, to be tolerated at best. Her sisters had seemed oblivious, involved in their friends and TV. They were enough older than Lynn that their worlds seldom crossed, either at school or later, when they were absorbed by their own families. After her sisters were away at school, her parents allowed her to have her own TV and phone, making them even more distant.

Not that there hadn't been good times when she was small.

She looked over at Del who seemed to know so clearly who she was—a black woman trying to make a life for her kids. Lynn knew she couldn't begin to imagine what that must be like. But at least Del had a mother and a family that clearly supported her goals and helped in her struggle.

Del was saying, "It looks like we might have another suspect. The neighbor—Arthur Collins. Turns out he hated Sam, quarreled with him often. They had a shouting match in the hallway, recently. He told us he wasn't in the hotel at the time of the murder. He claimed to have been out working for clients of his accounting business when Sam was killed. He goes out every day between one and four. Works at home the rest of the day, but he couldn't remember which clients he was working for."

"So does he have an alibi or not?"

A thundering sound took over from the next room. "Turn down the TV!" Del shouted. The noise was reduced marginally.

Del shut the door and sat down again. "We checked the clients from his computer entries. It seems they don't exist or have moved."

"What did he say? He must have known you would check."

"He was embarrassed and got defensive when we pointed out we couldn't find any clients. Blustered about how that wasn't any of our business. Then he went on about his mission from God to save us from ourselves and the Devil. He doesn't pretend he's not glad Sam is dead. He talks about the just punishment for Devil worship etc...."

"That's not what he told me." Lynn said.

Del sounded nonplussed. "Wouldn't you know. When did you talk to him?"

"Went back the day after the death to talk to the desk clerk, Nelson, who had been there when Sam came down the stairs. Collins was at the desk haranguing about how Sam deserved it. Thought I could get some background on Sam. Collins wanted me to print his version of reality, but gave me no real info. I gave him up as not of this world."

Del was thoughtful. "You don't think he did it?"

"It's true he didn't like Sam much. Does he know how to do drug stuff?"

"The job was bungled anyway. He could have figured out how to make it look like a drug overdose from the information in one of his tracts against drugs. When I talked to him he looked at his watch and consulted the calendar a lot. I think maybe he loses periods of time. He's with the shrinks now for a couple days of observation. One thing we did find out was that Sam was a member of the gang that attacked his mother."

It was Lynn's turn to be surprised. "My God, how did they end up in the same hotel?"

"Collins says he forgave Sam a long time ago, decided to convert him and followed him here."

"Did Sam spend time in jail?" Lynn asked.

"Sam was a minor at the time—got off with probation. The others went to jail for assault and attempted robbery. The woman was nearly eighty and she chased them down the street with some sort of souvenir World War I bayonet. Somebody did push her, probably to avoid getting stabbed, but she died of a

48

heart attack from overexertion. " Del chuckled. "That's the way I would like to go—chasing a bunch of punks at eighty."

"So why wait til now if he wanted revenge on Sam?"

"Sam didn't listen to Collins instead he joined the Devil worshipers," Del responded.

Lynn shook her head. "Doesn't seem very likely. So is Marta off the hook as a suspect?"

"For the time being, yes."

Lynn found herself very relieved. She told Del about the meeting at the old theater. About what Peter had said.

Del tried to reassure her. "I won't say he isn't on the right track. There are plenty of people on and off drugs in their organization, but as far as we know it's all rehab stuff."

"I haven't seen Marta since the meeting."

"I can see that doesn't make you happy." She sighed and got up to tell Danny to get ready for bed. When she got back she said, "I can't say it's not useful to us to have her in your apartment, but it looks to me as if you might be getting yourself in too deep with this woman, whatever her motives are."

"I can take care of myself. Anyway, there is nothing between us."

"Not yet, but you obviously wish there was."

• • •

The next day Lynn went to the Kalimaya's offices for her appointment with Mr. Singh. Unlike the theater, his office in a suburban mall was modern and newly furnished with the latest in tasteful decor. It reminded Lynn of a very expensive psychiatrist's waiting room. The only hint of the Society's religion was a large glass case in one corner full of Eastern religious antiques, mostly gods and goddesses—the kind generally seen only in museums. The sari-clad receptionist volunteered proudly, "That is part of Mr. Singh's private collection. It makes me miss my home country a little less." How was it that Mr. Singh could afford such a collection let alone obtain it? Here the concession to the spiritual was a simple altar in the corner with fresh flowers in front of a painting covered with a cloth in the Buddhist way.

Lynn was tentatively lifting the corner of the cloth when Mr.

Singh came in with the air of a hurried businessman. He came over and lifted the cover for her. Under it was an antique painting of a smiling, many-armed red goddess holding a bowl with blood spilling from it. Smiling almost conspiratorially at her he said. "A painting of Kali from the thirteenth century. I imagine she seems to you a terrible demoness, something out of one of your horror movies. Such an interpretation comes from your Western dichotomous way of thinking. But like all mothers Kali is the giver of life. That's what the bowl of blood symbolizes for us. Kali-ma also has the power to withhold life or take it away. She is all...."

"And she's the one that took Sam Jenson?"

He sat down at his desk and frowned at her with obvious disapproval in his voice. "A rather blunt way to describe an unfortunate occurrence. Certainly we teach that such defiance of the Goddess...that suicide is never a valid option to life's tests. "

"Did you see anything about his behavior that indicated he might be about to...'defy the Goddess?'"

"I was never Mr. Jenson's personal mentor. That was Marta's role. However I must say he seemed quite content with his life in our midst. Besides our spiritual guidance, we provide the family that many people have been deprived of. "

"Did he have any disagreements with other members, any enemies in the group?"

"I was not informed that this was to be a discussion of the circumstances of Mr. Jenson's unfortunate departure. I was informed that you are a reporter and was fully expecting to answer questions about our organization." He smiled rather reluctantly. "We believe that it is important to enlighten those misinformed about us at every opportunity. As you know, Mr. Jenson's death did not enhance our public image."

Lynn asked questions about the history and organization of the Society. He answered briefly and undefensively, but he quite deftly evaded anything she could not have gotten from her research into earlier newspaper articles. He pointed out the address of the Society's new mission on the written statement that he gave her. "I suggest you visit it and see the extensive good works we do before you publish your article."

Lynn was struck by the contrast with Mr. Singh's office as she walked into the Kalimaya Society's Mission, a crowded storefront full of people eating, juggling, sleeping and talking. Stacks of pamphlets and an old Xerox machine competed for space with an old wooden desk and a random assortment of unmatched chairs on the worn, paint-splashed floor. Among the workers stuffing envelopes and the street people waiting for attention, she didn't see anyone from the house where Marta had been living. When she asked for Marta, a woman finally turned from her job of sorting pamphlets to direct her up a rickety set of stairs.

Marta stood up when Lynn entered the small, dark office at the head of the stairs. She seemed nervous, distracted and surprised to see Lynn. Lynn explained the Mr. Singh had sent her.

Lynn could hear the anger in Marta's voice, as she apologized for the state of the mission. "We've started a retreat—on an estate that was given to us recently in the northern part of the state. It means that we have even fewer resources and people to work here than we did before. "

"Why didn't you come back last night?"

Marta closed the door, leaned against it and said, "You said no strings. I have responsibilities. I can't be explaining everything to you. Your behavior yesterday at the meeting makes it very difficult for me. I had to tell Mr. Singh that you're from a newspaper. It's bad enough that we have the misfortune of Sam's death...."

"My detective friends tell me they are zeroing in on a suspect."

Marta looked surprised."You mean they have given up on me? Who is it?"

"A neighbor, Mr. Collins. Seems Sam might have been responsible in the death of Mr. Collins' mother."

"That man may be a little crazy, but he's harmless, I'm sure. I know about that incident with his mother. Sam was just a neighborhood kid at the time. She died chasing him and his friends down the street. Mr. Collins knew that it wasn't Sam's fault. He wouldn't want to hurt Sam. Actually he was trying to...to save Sam's soul. Sam told me Collins was angry about his involvement with us. He worked too hard trying to convert Sam to have killed him."

"I agree with you, but Collins doesn't have an alibi. Says he doesn't remember which clients he was with. The police haven't been able to establish that he has any clients at all currently."

"I know where he probably was. He carries signs and pickets, gives sermons on the street. He pickets us all the time."

"Was he doing that at the time Sam died?"

Marta thought for a minute. "I don't remember seeing him on that day. But you didn't come here to talk about Mr. Collins."

"Mr. Singh wanted me to see some of the other aspects of your organization. It does seem as if you are trying here to do some necessary work. I would still like to interview your guru."

"Mr. Singh feels that we must protect her. It's true—she would talk to everyone—never stop. Her generosity is boundless. What is it that you want to write about us?"

"Your Mr. Singh gave you permission to be interviewed?" Lynn said caustically.

Marta sat down wearily. "He thinks I can convince you to let us speak for ourselves in a newspaper article. He wants some good publicity."

"I know. I just talked to him. It sounds as if you and Mr. Singh disagree about whether I'm capable of giving you good publicity."

Marta eyes were cold, resigned. "He told me to give you whatever information you need for an article about us."

"If I could get what I want—an interview with your leader, the one you call The Sister. I don't know why you resist letting me interview her. I thought she was the one who represented what you are. She's your leader, isn't she?"

Marta was silent. Then she said without looking at Lynn, "I could give you a statement from her, but your paper wouldn't print it. Not scandalous enough."

"I could try."

Marta's face flushed with anger. "Why should you? You don't know us and don't want to know."

"I want to know *you.* Doesn't that count for something?" At that Marta looked away. Lynn was sure she had blown it this time.

When Marta turned back, her face was impassive, and her voice no longer carried anger as she leaned forward to say, quietly, "I'll talk to you because the Sister said that you have a good heart and will be fair in your reporting. What might be between us has nothing to do with it."

So the Sister felt she could be trusted. Somehow the thought did not make Lynn comfortable.

Then Marta spoke fervently about the work of the Kalimayas. They had already started a small program in Hartfield to find housing and work as well as food for some of their less fortunate converts. They were trying to work with some of the city agencies, although that was difficult, not just because of the bureaucracy, but because of their religious orientation. Marta had set up some drug workshops which she ran herself.

Lynn followed Marta into a room where the Kalimayas were distributing clothing and food. The workers eyed Lynn nervously, but Marta gave them a reassuring smile as she took some photos. After they went back to her office Marta explained that the women were nervous because, though they were trained by the Society as counselors and nurse midwives, they did not have official sanction. The need was too great for them to wait for official pieces of paper.

But when Lynn began to ask more in-depth questions on that subject, Marta said coldly, "I would prefer that you not mention that in your article; we have enough trouble from the city officials and the police as it is."

• • •

Lynn wrote a brief, but positive article about the Society's social programs with a couple of human interest photos of homeless people who were being helped and a brief statement of principle that Marta said was a direct quote from the Sister.

5

The smell of hot spices reassured her even before she opened the door the next evening. Marta was in the kitchen, silently chopping vegetables. Lynn blurted out, "You saw the paper?"

Marta didn't look at her but nodded. A long sigh. "It was what I expected."

"I did my research...some people would kill for that kind of media attention...."

"Mr. Singh seemed pleased; we got the movie review he wanted instead of an article about our true purpose."

"And what is that, really? It's not that I haven't been trying to find out."

"I thought you understood." Marta dumped the vegetables in the hot oil as if the sizzling made a statement of her feelings. "The man who cannot trust sees only the dust of the road, and can go nowhere."

"News is about what is happening, not about what you want to happen. Anyway, I'm not a man."

Marta laughed then and looked at her. "So I have noticed." In the silence between them, soft brown eyes, the sight of full lips engulfed Lynn. It was as if the atmosphere grew white hot for a moment. Lynn wanted to reach out, but Marta turned away again to stir the steaming vegetables vigorously.

Lynn said in exasperation, "What did you want me to write?"

Marta turned off the burner, took the pan, scraped the veggies into a bowl, and put them on the table. She spooned rice into another bowl, then looked at Lynn silently for a moment. "The shell of a seed will not make a tree."

"You mean, if you can't say something good, don't say anything at all."

"No,I don't mean that." Marta sat down and put some food on her plate. Before she took a bite she said, "Always black or white. Isn't that what you feminists call dichotomous thinking?" Marta tried to eat but gave up in frustration. "I know you think the other members of the Society are agents of the Devil corrupting my pure and loving soul. You, the great white knight, will come to my rescue and carry me off to your castle while they burn in the righteous flame of your journalistic justice."

Lynn laughed outright. There was some truth in Marta's picture. She did want to save her. Maybe she even wanted the cult to be corrupt so that she could win Marta away. Had that been obvious in her article? She thought she'd let the pictures and the statements speak for themselves. Her commentary had been in the editing. The absurdity of some of Singh's statements did not require editorial comment. The Society's association with the world of drug users...so many ex-addicts as converts was obvious, but Marta was right. Maybe Lynn had editorialized too much.

Marta was suddenly far away, her anger dissipated. "I apologize. The truth is that I don't agree at all with Mr. Singh's interpretation of our way. Your article did rather straightforwardly state his point of view. It's not your fault, really. We've been so busy trying to set up our Mission, we haven't had the time to work out our differences. That's really why we agreed not to publish an interview with The Sister. It would be completely misinterpreted—misunderstood. Journalism doesn't lend itself to philosophical and ethical discourse; even you will have to admit. I appreciate that you went out on a limb for us and published Singh's statement. I know it was hard on you and your journalist's agenda—and your prejudices. And I know you did it to please me. But remember, you promised no strings. Being here causes conflict for me too. You must understand that if you push, I can't stay here."

Lynn blushed. It was true she had hoped a positive article would not only please Marta but might well ease off the pressure for Marta to move out. Why was she cursed with such a crush on a woman who was married to her religious ideology as well as her missionary cause. Suddenly Lynn did not have the heart to argue her case. She had no energy for another discussion of the feminist implication of the ideology of the Kalimaya Society.

They ate in silence.

After supper Marta left without further comment.

• • •

During the next two weeks Lynn kept her doubts to herself. She had new stories to follow up; she couldn't afford to get so involved. In the evenings, over supper, she would talk about her most recent article with Marta and ask general questions about her day. Marta would answer in generalities and jargon. "The weakness of the flesh and spirit—a prayer to Lakshmi to lighten the burdens of the lost. If only the spirit of Durga in each of us would rise up, the buffalo demon could be slain. But he always seemed to reappear too quickly."

In the silent empty apartment, when Marta was gone to some Kalimaya meeting or other, Lynn would begin to wonder what Marta really was? Where did she go when she left Lynn's sight? Why wouldn't she share her concerns and worries with Lynn? Who was this woman?

But when Marta was there, always in control, calm, nearly beatific in her wisdom, Lynn wanted to trust her. She envied Marta's devotion and her belief that she could solve problems just with enough effort. Sitting across the table from Marta while they ate she felt content, happy. A word, a touch was almost enough. More and more there were those moments when Lynn could believe they were becoming lovers. If Marta weren't so preoccupied; if Lynn weren't so busy; if the right moment, the right atmosphere; if....

• • •

On Sunday a friend called with a story she had heard from Lynn's ex, Shirley, about the weirdos she had seen at Lynn's apartment when she had gone there to retrieve a record. The apartment had been full of people on an afternoon when Lynn was at work. "Shirley said they were a bunch of glassy-eyed hippy-druggies playing strange music. I didn't know whether Shirl was being spiteful because she was jealous of your new lady or if we should worry that you've gone off the deep end."

That afternoon she went home early. The hall was silent as

she approached her door, but the door was unlocked. She went in quietly. Marta might be meditating.

There were empty plates on the table, a strange smell—onion and incense? She went into Shirl's old room. There they were in a circle, a strange collection of people, but no Marta. Had she just now brought them in from the street? A woman with scraggly gray hair, a long haired workman with a gold earring, still in his paint covered overalls, a man in a business suit, a teenage girl with a partially shaved head. All were sitting on the floor in silence. Homeless people? Drug addicts? Several pairs of eyes shone on her silently in the darkened room. She asked where Marta was and no one answered her. She walked out pulling the door carefully closed behind her and went back to work.

What would she say? Knowing she would have to confront Marta about this, she found herself rehearsing her questions and couldn't concentrate on work.

That evening when she walked through the door Marta was putting flower petals in the little basket she used for her offerings. She looked up with sad eyes. "I'm sorry. I should have asked."

"Please tell me what's going on."

"It's just that the others won't let me use the communal space at the house. We have our differences about who is ready to join us, who we should admit to our circle. There's absolutely no quiet space at the mission. Singh won't tolerate us in his counseling rooms. He doesn't want substance-contaminated people. He says it muddies the spirit fields."

"And you don't think I care who wanders in and out of *my* apartment? Who are those people anyway? What are they doing that your glassy eyed brethren can't tolerate them?"

"Singh and Jason and some others feel it's too risky to work with those who might need a lot of material or even psychiatric help. I'm sure I'll be able to persuade them; it's just a matter of time."

"You mean that some of them are still on drugs? Why not send them to a rehab center, or are they not ready to give up their habit?"

Marta looked down at the red petals in her hand. "I won't

pretend that some of them aren't people in serious trouble. Some of them *have* gotten trapped by drugs. It's a six-month waiting period, if you are lucky, to get into a rehab center even if you have some resources. But it's not your problem. If you don't want them here I won't bring them, but our resources are so limited."

Lynn felt guilty suddenly. Here was Marta making sacrifices to help these people and she, herself wasn't even willing to share her living room. She took Marta's hand and squeezed it gently. Of course she didn't doubt Marta's good intentions. She took a deep breath. "As a journalist I keep track of people in trouble, but that usually doesn't involve bringing them home for therapy. Not to mention that I could lose my job."

Marta put the offering on the altar, lit a candle and muttered a few words under her breath. Then she turned and said, rather stiffly, "I'll find somewhere else tomorrow."

Lynn gave in then and shook her head in resignation, "I know, I'm not even here during the daytime; there's no reason not to meet. Let's just hope the cops and my boss don't notice."

Marta smiled and gave Lynn a hug. "I'm sorry. I should have talked to you. I'll find a place for my gatherings soon so you wouldn't have to be bothered."

6

Del called her at work the next week. "Collins has gone stone uncooperative; he won't talk to us or his lawyer. He keeps saying you promised to do an article based on your interview. Maybe he'll open up to you if you go see him again."

"I'll be down this afternoon."

"He isn't at the Hotel. Because of the psychiatrist's report the judge felt it was best to house him in the state hospital at least temporarily. Since his mother is dead and we can't locate any other family we contacted his ex-wife. She refuses to have anything to do with him."

"They think he's certifiable?"

Del sighed, "It looks that way, right now. He wasn't making much sense, even when he was talking."

"Did you get a confession then?"

"Not exactly, and we probably couldn't use it anyway, if he's suffering from delusions. There is no hard evidence against him. He has motive and no alibi, and at times he seems to think he could have done it."

When Lynn got to the state hospital, Arthur Collins was sitting on his bed in the narrow room looking out the window onto the grounds.

His thermos was there on the dresser with his china cups. Lynn looked at her watch. It was after four. She pulled the end table toward him and set the cups out, pouring him tea.

He stared at her hands for a long time. She waited. He said, finally, "You should take better care of your nails."

She pulled away her hands, and he looked up. "She had hands like yours except that she took care of them—nicely rounded nails with just the barest polish. In very good taste." He

59

took a sip of tea, didn't seem to mind that it was barely warm.

"Your mother?"

He shook his head, no. "Linda. She was thin like you too—about your age, maybe younger. You should let your hair grow—not cut it so short. Hers was shiny and wavy too but lighter."

"Did she pass away too?"

"You might say that. She's dead to me. I told her not to marry that man." He looked away.

"Your daughter?"

He looked at Lynn startled. "My wife didn't want children. Linda was my sister."

A married sister. That's why they couldn't find her.

"Why didn't you tell your lawyer you had a sister? She could help you."

"Don't you tell them about her. I don't want her here."

"You're in a lot of trouble, Mr. Collins. The police suspect that you might have killed Sam. You can use all the help you can get. You don't have an alibi. The police can't find any of your clients. Where were you if you didn't kill him?"

"Whatever happens, it's God's will." He sat up, his voice strong , but trembling now. "I follow God's commandments."

"Like an eye for an eye?"

He glanced at Lynn briefly. He still held himself firmly in control, but the confidence was gone. A frown of confusion replaced it and he answered in a quiet voice. "I don't remember trying to kill him. Could I have done it?" He gripped his teacup tightly and searched Lynn's face as if for his own memory.

• • •

When she got home that evening she found Marta wrapped up in a quilt on the couch. Lynn knelt down by the quiet shape. The eyes fluttered open. They were red rimmed and there was a cut and the beginnings of a bruise on Marta's cheek. Lynn could feel her anger surge. "Who hit you?"

Marta frowned. "It doesn't matter now." She sat up. "Sorry about supper. I fell asleep."

"What happened? Was it that juggler?"

"You mean Jason? No, there was just a minor incident, a disagreement not worthy of reporting in your paper."

Lynn was stung. "Is that what you still really think of me? That all I care about is getting a good story? I got the impression that we had gotten to know each other better than that."

"We are opposites. You and I—that's all. You reporters look for the sordid in people's lives and we try to find the good so as to help them find a true path. Sometimes that's very hard. This was just one of my bad days."

Lynn stood to hide her hurt feelings. "If you think me such a terrible person, why did you accept my invitation to live here? You knew I was a reporter from the first." There, it was out, the question she had been wanting to ask since Marta had arrived.

Marta didn't look at her. "I guess Jason is right. I'm too trusting, naive, incapable of practical thinking." She pulled the quilt tighter around herself and shivered, though the room seemed too warm to Lynn. "I'll move tomorrow, not burden you anymore. Jason will be happy that I don't have any place to meet my 'addicts and queers.' That is if you don't mind my sleeping here one more night."

Lynn felt a door slam in her head. She marched into the kitchen, took some vegetables from the refrigerator and began chopping them for a salad.

Marta followed, the blanket still wrapped around her. "I'm sorry. Things are just so difficult now. Every organization has its internal disagreements. It doesn't help feeling threatened with everything paraded in public if I say the wrong thing or get misinterpreted."

"Your organization is rather flamboyant. Isn't that because you want publicity? Why is it so surprising that the media is interested?"

Marta avoided the question. "I need to ask you not to write anything more, at least until we get this settled."

"What settled?"

Again Marta didn't answer. Lynn looked at her. Such a pathetic bundle, the bruised face peering out from behind the blue and white quilt. Lynn went over and put her arms around Marta.

Her voice came muffled, from beneath the blanket. "It's better if you don't know what our problems are. Then I won't have to ask you not to tell the truth."

Her heart pounding, Lynn released her and looked into her face. "You haven't answered my question. Why did you accept my offer?"

There was detectable anger in Marta's voice as she said, "That was what you wanted, wasn't it? I saw it in your eyes the moment you walked up to me. Like those people who come to our meetings and want a perfect answer, a perfect religion, perfect happiness. I could see you saw a kind of perfection in me. I just tried to give you as much of that as I could manage."

Lynn could not trust herself to speak yet.

Marta was also silent for a moment. Then she said very quietly. "Do you think I haven't known that you want us to become lovers? Jason thinks that we are."

"Then why...? Is that why he—"

"No! And he was never my lover. I am sorry if you're feeling deceived. It is hard enough to be...oneself when one feels so strongly what others need. I had hoped you would understand...."

"You certainly seemed to know a lot about me at one glance."

"The Sister says it is a weakness of mine—seeing people's needs and trying to help them find what they want."

"What *you* think they want. And what do you want?"

Marta shook her head, the tears running across her bruised cheek. "I don't know. I thought I knew once—then you showed up, complicating things." She tried to smile. "Perhaps I want a kind of perfection too."

Lynn couldn't hide her own anger. It was worse because she could feel the truth in what Marta said. "And that perfection is to be found in the Kalimaya Society with people who hit you... not to mention the homophobia."

Marta threw off the blanket and stormed out of the kitchen. Lynn followed her, helpless. "And that's the end of the conversation?"

"You have misunderstood everything. I accepted your offer because I truly needed less...involvement. Sam's death... I can't help feeling it was my fault."

"What if I told you I just want to know you and love you the way you really are?"

"I wouldn't believe you. I'm not separate from the Kalimaya

Society. I am part of what you call a cult. Right now it's my life. It's who I am." Marta covered her face for a moment with her fingers pressed against the bridge of her nose. Then she said quietly as from far away, "I will be leaving town soon. I have been assigned elsewhere. That will mean you can keep your perfection always." Marta saw the immediate pain in Lynn's eyes. She smiled and said, "That is one way to be part of the Goddess, you see. You will know only the godly part of me. It is the only gift I can give. It is all I have to give."

Lynn opened her mouth to speak. The dam of anger and hurt had begun to break. Marta saw the tears and kissed Lynn's eyes to stop the flow.

This was going to be all. Soon Marta would be gone. Lynn understood the message. There was to be no time wasted on recriminations. She pulled away from Marta and went to wash her face and try to restore her dignity. She was determined that if Marta was leaving, Lynn would treat her simply as a temporary guest. She certainly did not want the woman's emotional charity—kissing away her tears as if Lynn were a little girl who had bruised her knee.

And, now that there was no keeping Marta, what reason was there not to pursue the article that Gale really wanted?

When she reemerged Marta had dinner underway. They ate in silence. After dinner Lynn put down her cup of tea and asked abruptly, "Can you get me an appointment with her?"

"Who?"

"The one you call the Sister?"

"Can't you leave it alone?"

"No."

"What do you really want to know?"

"What does Sam's death have to do with your group's present controversy?"

"Not mincing words now I see." Marta said dryly.

Lynn remained silent, waiting, once again the good investigator.

"As far as I know, there is no connection except that some of Sam's old buddies in the drug trade might have resented our getting him on the straight and narrow."

"Do you know any of those old buddies?"

"It's hard to avoid some contact with dealers when we're trying to save some of the victims. I know some by sight."

"Are some of them among your converts?"

"Not that I am aware of."

"How about donations?"

"What do you mean?"

"I mean, is it possible that some of your larger financial patrons could be connected with the drug trade? Is that the mysterious controversy that got you beat up? Do some of your organizational leaders want to accept tainted money?"

Marta silently took her dishes to the sink and began washing them.

Lynn stood behind her. "If your membership is so pure, why can't you talk to me?"

Marta carefully dried her hands not looking at Lynn. Then she headed for the study.

Lynn followed her. "What does this stuff, this group, these people do for you really?"

"There is more to life than VCRs and sex," Marta said over her shoulder.

"You think I don't know that?"

"You aren't ready for some kinds of wisdom."

"You mean you won't talk to me."

"Talk to Jason or one of the others. Get your interview with the Sister. They can give you answers to your questions as well as I can."

"You mean your cover story."

"If you like." Marta went to the closest dragged out her duffel bag and began stuffing her things in it.

Lynn suddenly felt panicky. "Come on. I didn't say I was going to write anything more."

Marta turned and looked straight at Lynn. "One of the illusions one is always falling into is that one can change people."

Lynn's head was spinning. Was she really about to lose Marta? Until this moment she hadn't understood how much she wanted her to stay. But she couldn't speak. She just stood watching as Marta struggled with the string on her bag. It felt to Lynn as if Marta were moving in slow motion—a nightmare of slowness.

Anger helped Lynn find words. "My newspaper mind did record the statement that your stay was temporary. But you didn't say you would leave in the middle of the night without any explanation." Lynn moved toward her, wanting to touch her—stop her. But Marta went to the door quickly, her bag in tow.

Now Lynn was furious. "Come on. What illegal stuff are your cult buddies into that you're so frightened? Was it one of them who did in Sam?"

Marta turned and again looked directly at her. "They were right. It's best that I go now. I'm done with those who can't trust. Play with your cameras and your computer all you like. I won't help you. I have more important work."

But before she closed the door she hesitated and turned one last time, her voice hushed. "One day you'll be very, very glad that you don't have to share my truths." Then she closed the door quickly.

7

*L*ynn came home early the next day from work feeling a little crazy. She even imagined that she would find Marta back. She walked in and stood staring at her cluttered living room that now felt so empty. She made herself a cup of tea, then sat on the couch staring at the wall.

She scolded herself. No, it was not an empty room. She had filled it herself with things that she loved. How long ago? But pre-Marta time seemed like a thousand years ago.

Walking around the room, she collected every evidence of Marta's presence. The ancient paperback translation of the Bhagavad-Gita, a few outdated flyers for meetings of the Society, one silver earring with the post missing. She rearranged the furniture so it was exactly the way it had been before Marta came—took the plants Marta had started and threw them out.

Then she stood before the little altar on top of the bureau in the corner. A white cloth napkin protected the wood. On it was a small wooden bowl with flower petals still damp from the water sprinkled on them, and a thin stick of incense stuck into the rice paste offering, ready to be lit. She threw the whole mess into the trash. She opened all the windows, mopped the kitchen floor and threw out all the leftovers, She discarded all Marta's spices and all her teas, so there would be no hint of her left.

But the next day she couldn't find the strength to go to work. After she called in sick, all she could manage was to curl up on the sofa in the morning sun. She began remembering how much she had loved this room where in winter the sunlight touched almost every corner sometime during the day.

She stayed there all day and finally got up only to pour herself a glass of whiskey, straight. Maybe that would help. She sat drinking it until the last of the afternoon sun touched a bright spot of color sticking out of the drawer in the table by the door. She went to open it. Marta's blue paisley shawl. How had she missed that yesterday? Strange she had been so intent on details, but hadn't seen it.

She picked up the shawl and closed the drawer. The sunlight showed scratches in the surface of the table. Funny—when she had purchased that table, she hadn't noticed the scratches. She had seen only the curling pattern of the grain, tight yet flowing. Now she saw the flaws. Had she missed Marta's flaws too, by seeing only what she wanted to see?

In some part of her mind she knew that someday the room would feel full again even if Marta never came back. She wrapped the paisley shawl around herself and curled up on the sofa.

• • •

In the next weeks Lynn threw herself into her work determined to forget about Marta. She even avoided asking Del about the case and whether she knew where Marta was, but nothing seemed to help.

More weeks passed, but Lynn still could not get Marta out of her thoughts. When she finally went to the mission to look for her, the receptionist told her that Marta had gone to Nepal on a meditative retreat and had left no forwarding address. Lynn handed the woman her press card and asked to talk with someone else. While she waited she noted that the place looked very different. It wasn't just the new furniture, the freshly painted walls, the rather neutral spiritual posters. Partitions had been built so that there were now separate offices and a waiting room. It felt more like a doctor's office than a mission. The few 'clients' waiting there looked more upscale too.

Soon she was ushered into one of the offices by the receptionist. It was Nancy, the woman who had argued with Marta when she had first moved in with Lynn, sitting behind the desk. But this time Nancy welcomed Lynn with a rather over-sweet smile.

Lynn smiled back. "The place looks wonderful. You must have found a very generous donor."

Did Nancy look uncomfortable for a moment? All she said was. "What can we do for you today?"

67

When Lynn told her she wanted to find Marta, Nancy said, "Even the Sister agrees Marta was not focusing on her mission here with the proper concentration. We all thought she needed some time off to sort out her priorities. She is meditating—a retreat."

Lynn asked for her address.

Again the oversweet smile. Lynn couldn't help feeling the triumphant spite behind that smile as Nancy said, "She doesn't have an address exactly, being up in the mountains, but if you'll bring us a letter, the next person going to Nepal will take it for you."

When she got back to her office she called Del. Sam Jenson's death had become another of those 'continuing cases' in Del and Rog's open files. Mr. Collins was staying on at the home since they still had not located his sister.

Del told her that as far as she could determine Marta had indeed gone to Nepal—to work on the retreat the Kalimaya Society was developing there, but Mr. Singh had reassured Del that Marta would come back if it was necessary to testify. Del didn't have an address either.

None of it helped Lynn. She felt as if there was still an open file on their relationship. Without much hope she went back and left a letter at the mission—to be forwarded, but got no answer.

• • •

It was a cool night in late September. Though she no longer thought about her during the day, Lynn was dreaming, as she often did, of Marta. In this dream Marta, dressed in a huge blue-green taffeta ball gown, was in the kitchen chopping vegetables with a cleaver, hitting the cutting board in her usual vigorous way.

Lynn woke to the sound of knocking on the door. Who would be here this late? It was after eleven p.m. Sleepily she opened the door a crack, leaving the safety chain on. Standing outside were two typical young business men, one in a dark gray suit, the other in navy blue with thoroughly polished shoes. Lynn guessed the one in the gray suit to be East Indian.

Gray suit said, "Marta Handley? May we come in please and speak with you?" Lynn explained that Marta no longer was living there and asked what they wanted.

The Indian persisted, smiling as if he did not believe her, "We wish only to make an offer to you, a legitimate contract." He held out a card. "J. Hijras here."

She took it through the crack left by the chain. It had the name, Asia Imports, under the image of a tiger. The names Gruber and Allen were printed in one corner and there was a telephone number and a downtown address in the other. J. Hijras had written his name on the back.

"I'm not Marta. She really doesn't live here any more."

Blue suit spoke up then. "She wrote to us that she was interested in working with us...importing...of local craft items—on her trips into Nepal and India. She was to contact some manufacturers there for us in connection with the retreat in Nepal and its...handicraft program, of course."

J. Hijras smiled. "You wouldn't have a forwarding address for her by any chance?"

"Isn't it a little late for business calls?" Lynn didn't like the way he was trying to look past her into the loft as if he expected Marta to be hiding in the corners.

"We apologize for the inconvenience. We were in the area for the evening and...if you will just let us come in and talk to you for a moment."

"Contact her organization." She tried to close the door.

Sticking his foot in the door, Hijras said, "We know she was living here. All we want is a forwarding address. It will be important for her and her...organization."

Lynn didn't like this slimy persistence. "Why don't you contact the Kalimaya Society directly? They aren't hard to find."

Blue suit said, "Look here, we are actually from the Immigration Department. We have reason to think Marta and her organization are harboring illegal aliens."

J. Hijras piped in when Lynn didn't respond. "She may be illegal herself. Her mother was Nepalese. We just want to check."

"Let me see your credentials," Lynn demanded, "or I'm calling the police."

Blue suit turned on the charm then. "No need to be alarmed. It's just a routine check. She isn't in any danger of arrest."

Hijras pushed his leg further in the door and tried to reach around to unlatch the chain, but Lynn kicked his leg out trapping his hand. With a yelp he pulled it out and she locked the door.

She heard them retreat down the hallway. She went to call Del, although they would be long gone before the cops could do anything. What did she have to charge them with? It would be her word against theirs. Marta again—the woman was haunting her. Suddenly she was exhausted.

Del thought she was checking in about Mr. Collins. "We found his sister, Linda, living in Ohio, married with two nearly grown kids. Hadn't seen her brother for ten years. Nice lady though, even though dear Arthur disowned her for marrying an atheist. Mr. Collins got a small inheritance from his mother and he did not share it. The sister didn't argue. We still haven't located any of his clients, but it doesn't look—"

"It's not him I'm worried about. It's Marta. Two guys just came snooping for her. Almost muscled through my door."

"What can you tell me about them?

"One of the guys gave me a card."

"Give me the info and we'll run a check on them."

"He said his name was Hijras. The card says Gruber and Allen—Asia Imports—" Lynn heard a knock. "Just a minute, someone is at the door again. Hold on."

Lynn opened the door a crack, nervously expecting the two men again, but quickly unlatched the chain, in shock. Marta slipped through, her eyes dark with fear. She had nothing with her, not even a sweater against the chill fall night and she was shivering. Lynn said to Del, "Talk to you later."

Lynn wanted to put her arms around the shivering body. Instead she led her to the couch and wrapped a quilt around her. "What's going on? What are you afraid of? They told me you were in Nepal."

"I was there, until today. They brought me back for a meeting...I'm not supposed to have come here...not supposed to see you, but I—" Marta covered her face with the quilt. Lynn realized she was crying and held her quietly until the sobs stopped. Then she dared to ask, "Why did you leave the way you did and why didn't you answer my letter?"

Marta looked up from the blanket. "I never got any letter."

Lynn couldn't bear the sight of her thin, tear streaked face. She whispered, "You can't know how much I've missed you."

"I wanted you to forget about me. I wanted you to be angry so you would not miss me."

Lynn hid her face in the dark fragrant hair.

Marta took Lynn's hand in her own and said, "You were so good to me. I hated leaving you that way. I thought if I was nasty enough you would forget me, and I could get on with what I had to do. It didn't work. Lies never work. I'm glad I have a chance to tell you how...grateful I am for the help you gave me."

The woman was admitting that she cared. "Grateful isn't the point. It's nice to know—"

"Whatever you might think, my leaving had nothing to do with my feelings for you. It was good for me to be here with you. It was just that, well, we all felt I needed a little time to meditate, in a quiet place—a real retreat. Decide what I had to do. Too many voices were pushing me this way and that."

Lynn was overwhelmed by the warmth now shining through the tears in Marta's brown eyes. All the loss and anger she had suffered the last months seemed like nothing and all she wanted was that soft slender body, that satin skin, warm next to hers.

But Lynn suddenly remembered the men who had come looking for Marta. Should she tell Marta they were there? Just one more thing to frighten her?

"Just one question that bothers me right now."

Marta looked into her eyes.

"You're a U.S. citizen, right? You were born here?"

Marta looked puzzled. "You can't mean that only people born in the great mysterious East have the ability to believe in the spiritual?" She smiled. "Religion as geographical, a disease theory, or maybe genetic?" Marta stared at her waiting, a question and a smile in her eyes.

"There were two men here looking for you just a little while ago. They said they were from Immigration. But when I asked for identification, they hedged."

The fear darkened her eyes again. "What did they look like?"

"Usual dark suits, shiny shoes, I think one was from India."

"What did you tell them?"

"I said you weren't here. I shut the door in their faces."

"What else did they say?"

"Well, at first they claimed to be in the import business, Asia Imports, some guy named Hijras gave me a card. At first he said he wanted to talk to you about importing crafts through the retreat in Nepal." Lynn got the card.

Marta examined it nervously and there was fear in her voice. "I doubt Hijras was his real name. It means gay, effeminate man in Hindi. Maybe it was just his personal joke. There is a company, Gruber and Allen—a couple of businessmen that have approached the Society—about importing gems and fabric mostly. At one time we talked about bringing in stones to finance our work. There is no import duty on uncut gems; Nepal is a favored nation, you know. I have never met them. I wouldn't even recognize them; Singh was the one who has talked to them. He says they are legitimate."

"Just because these guys had their card doesn't mean that's who they are. Why are you afraid? Why did these guys come here looking for you just now that you are back?"

"Someone must have said I was back—at the mission. This was my last address before I left."

"But why are you afraid of them?"

Marta was silent. Then she said, not looking at Lynn, "What happened to all those pictures you took at the meeting you came to?"

Lynn shrugged. "Why?"

"It's not important. Throw them away."

"You didn't answer my question. Why are you afraid?"

Marta drew away from Lynn shivered and wrapped the blanket tighter around her arms. "I've been talking to people, saying what had to be said."

"Like Sam did?"

Marta shook her head. "He started out on the wrong side. He was a pawn. When he wanted to expose them he got caught. The same knights and bishops have me checkmated right now as far as the Kalimaya Society is concerned, but I have never cooperated in any illegal operation."

"But maybe someone in your organization is cooperating with the people that killed Sam. He didn't tell you who any of these people are?"

"I know what you think, but my spiritual companions aren't common criminals. They also are just pieces pushed around by invisible players. I've been trying to find out who those players are. I'm afraid, because I am getting close. Let me stay here, at least a few days. When I'm sure of what I suspect, I'll let you write it all."

"Someone in you organization has to know who they are. I'm going to call Del. This is something for the police to deal with. She can help you, you know. She's a friend."

"She is also a cop. We can handle things ourselves. It will be so much better that way." Marta voice was uncharacteristically harsh, but then she put a hand on Lynn's arm. "Please don't. They'll just arrest the wrong people. A lot of our members could be hurt needlessly. Believe me, these men are practical people. When the Society tells them we won't cooperate in any way, they'll go elsewhere. When we stick together we can't be intimidated."

"But right now you don't have that agreement. Is that it? There are some in your organization who don't want to tell them to go away. What is it that they are into—importing drugs? You think this has something to do with Asia Imports?"

"I don't know yet. We need income to support our work in Nepal. Allen and Gruber's proposal seems to be a legitimate alternative. All I have right now are my suspicions and what Sam told me about them."

Lynn sighed and held Marta closer. Here in her arms was the very woman she had been trying to exorcise from her life. Marta must know how angry she had been, but here she was asking to step back into Lynn's life—and asking for help. "And what then, after you have persuaded your spiritual buddies they must take a firm stand against the forces of evil? Will you really finally talk to me and even Del—fill us in on what's been going on, tell us what Sam told you about Allen and Gruber or will you just disappear again after a couple of days?"

Marta shivered. "Give me until tomorrow evening at least. Once I have the Society's agreement, you can call your cop friends and I'll tell them what I know."

"And then you'll leave."

73

Marta began to cry again silently, her body quivering under the quilt. Lynn went to boil water for tea.

When she came back, Marta was curled up in the quilt staring into the blackness outside the window. Lynn sat down next to her and took Marta's hands, warming her fingers in her own. Marta hid her face against Lynn's neck and said, "You were right about one thing; I can't let their silent and spoken messages about my sexuality rule my life. It's something about them that won't be easy to change. I can't wait for that to happen."

Lynn lifted Marta's face to hers and kissed her lips gently. They melted together, lost in the explosion of that gentle touch.

Then Lynn was suddenly pulled out of her blissful state by the silence of the tea kettle that had finally stopped whistling and she hurried in to save it from total destruction. She started another pot and went back to Marta on the couch.

Marta smiled and whispered, "Still no strings?"

"One or two maybe. I'll settle for a promise."

"Yes."

"Promise you won't leave again so suddenly. At least not without an explanation and a forwarding address."

Marta kissed her. "I can promise that at least."

A few minutes later the phone rang. They didn't answer it for a long time, but the ringing persisted.

It was Del. "The import guys check out. They really do have an office and proper paperwork. I have no clue why they were interested in Marta or why they were so pushy. You're sure you haven't heard from her? Who was that at the door?"

Del knew something was up. Marta's liquid brown eyes appealed to her to keep silent. Lynn covered the mouthpiece. "It's Del. What can I tell her?"

Marta pulled at Lynn with the passion in her eyes. Then she sighed and looked away. "Please don't say anything until after tomorrow's meeting. I can't stay a part of the Society if they work with the people that might have been responsible for Sam's death. I think they will agree not to cooperate, but, in any case, I promise, I'll give Del a statement about what I know then."

Lynn turned back to the phone. "Thanks Del. I'll call you if I hear anything."

Then it was Lynn's turn to shiver, this time with electric

excitement as she settled silently into the miracle of Marta—her scent, her silky hair, her magic touch. All of her doubts dissolved as their bodies revealed what words had never been able to express.

That night, after the wonder of their lovemaking, Lynn held Marta till she fell asleep, not wanting to let go of the euphoria, remembering each moment, wanting to feel the glow forever.

Forever lasted about thirty minutes, when a question began to nag her—a piece of the puzzle didn't fit. Why had Marta told her to throw away the pictures she had taken of the meeting at the theater? She had only made a few prints from all the negatives. She hadn't even bothered to make a contact print.

Finally her curiosity won out and she got up to make contacts of the negatives. The pictures were quite good, better than she had hoped. There was Marta on stage, beautiful as ever. She made some prints, keeping only the best. The negatives and one contact sheet went back into her shoe-box filing system. A second contact and the extra prints went into the bulging bag of trash which she tied up and took down to the basement. The rest of the prints she left to dry on her rigged line over the bathroom sink.

8

The next morning, Detective Roger Thomas came by her office, sat in her chair, lit a cigarette and put his feet on her desk. He had something on his mind. Lynn opened the window. "I thought you gave that up."

"I did. At least once a week." He flicked an ash into the wastebasket. "Del probably told you. We checked out the lead on Collins' alibi. Seems you were right. People saw somebody in Collins' usual get-up, wearing a Moses beard. He thinks nobody knows who he is. Not that they'd care. Typical paranoia. Unless somebody else was preaching in his get-up, your Indian roommate is back on the top of the key-suspect list." He looked at Lynn over his glasses.

Lynn turned her head away to hide her concern. What was Thomas after? Did he somehow know that Marta was back in Lynn's apartment? "She's not from India; she is a U. S. citizen, born in this country. Her mother was from Nepal. Are you planning to arrest her?" She paused and turned to look at him. "Do you know where she is?"

He shook his head. "We have reason to believe she is in the area though. There is a major meeting of the Kalimaya leadership happening today. You going to tell me where she is?"

Lynn turned to look at him. "Come on, Rog, what do you want me to say? Is there some new evidence? I thought she had an alibi."

He sat up and put out his cigarette. "I think those stars in your eyes are keeping your brain from working. You're a smart cookie. At least you used to be."

"Why would she kill Sam Jenson? What could she possibly have to gain?"

"Some very good people have gotten into trouble in order to finance their causes. Del told me that you are on to something."

"Some guys came looking for Marta. They seemed awful sure she was at my place. That's all I know right now."

"I'll bet it is." He got up. "Anyway, we think she's small potatoes even if she did do in Sam, but be careful. I'd hate to lose you to some sleazy drug organization. And keep in touch."

Lynn called her apartment as soon as he left. It was all she could do not to run home to make sure Marta was there. The phone call was a compromise.

Marta answered. "Lynn Evan's residence."

The sound of her voice made Lynn want to laugh with pleasure. "Anything I can bring you this evening?"

There was a silence at the other end. Then Marta said, relief clearly in her voice, "Lynn, I am glad it's you. Don't take too long coming home after work. I have some things I need talk to you about. Your friend Del called. I think she recognized my voice."

It was Lynn's turn to be silent for a moment. Who had Marta been afraid might be on the other end of the line? Did she dare mention that Marta was a suspect again? She decided it wasn't worth upsetting her. After all there was no new evidence. "I'll come home now."

"Not necessary. I have to go to the meeting. Don't worry. I'm coming back to your apartment. You'll see me this evening. I promise"

"It's not that I don't believe you. I'm just worried about you."

"I have to have time to get the issues resolved one way or the other. I will need your help then."

"OK, but be careful."

There was a sad laugh at the other end of the phone. Lynn couldn't tell what it meant. "I will be careful, full of care. That's what I am, always, meditation and prayer notwithstanding, full of care. You hit it on the nose."

Marta's tone worried Lynn, so she said, "Stay there. I'll be right over."

"No, I won't be here. Remember your promise. Tonight I'll tell you everything." She hung up the phone before Lynn could say anything more. Lynn went back to work reluctantly.

The first thing Lynn noticed when she came in that evening

was that Marta wasn't there. She looked hurriedly around the apartment for signs of her—a note, even an empty tea cup. Something about the room disturbed her. Everything was so neat. Marta had never done that. She had never touched Lynn's possessions. It was as if someone very orderly had searched the room. Everything had been carefully put back in its place, but too neatly. Even her shirt was folded neatly on the couch.

In the corner where Marta's altar had once been was a crude tiny basket woven from the dead leaves of one of Lynn's house plants, red geranium petals, and a few grains of rice. The floor was damp. For a moment Lynn imagined that it was blood. It seemed as if it was just water, though the rug was awfully wet, soapy as if someone had tried to clean up. She looked again for a message from Marta—nothing.

Had Marta really left again...without a good-bye? But she had promised. Surely, she would be back. Lynn had agreed not to talk to the police. Now she was sure that had been a mistake.

She called the office of the Kalimaya Society. There was no answer, not even an answering machine. How long should she wait before calling Del?

When Marta didn't show up by seven, Lynn finally called Del. "You probably realize already, Marta was here. Rog was right, she came for that meeting. She promised to talk to me about what has been going on with the Kalimayas—after the meeting. I'm worried; she hasn't come back yet...and...the apartment feels...strange."

Del was furious. "You should have called me right away. Anything missing from your apartment?" she snapped.

"What do you mean?"

"Maybe somebody came back after something."

"I don't understand."

"She's a murder suspect. Maybe there was something she left there that she didn't want found."

"I threw out everything when she left the first time."

"She doesn't know that. We've kept track of your Marta. She's been traveling, other cities, other countries—Nepal—to the retreat there. We think she organized this meeting. We are convinced it has a lot to do with the reason for Sam's murder. She flew in yesterday along with Kalimaya leaders from everywhere. We put a tail on her after she left your apartment this afternoon. Rog was planning to pick her up for questioning after the meeting, but she lost us after she left."

"When was it over?"

"Marta and a couple of others left at five; the rest are still there as far as I know."

Lynn tried to control the anxiety in her voice. "Why didn't you call me?"

Del was breathless with anger. "I hadn't noticed that you were being upfront with me. You going to tell me what's going on now?"

"Let's give her another hour. I'll call you when she gets here."

There was an outraged silence on the other end of the phone.

After she hung up she picked up the little basket. Why this? It wasn't like something that Marta would have made. The red petals from her geranium plant were carefully arranged in a bed of stems and leaves, so neat, yet it must have been constructed in a hurry. Where had she seen that before? Then she remembered the image of Sam's body with the leaves and petals clutched in his hand. Someone had made this one from what was at hand—the dead stems and petals of a house plant. Had that been a token from Marta—or someone else?

She stared at the red petals, the edges curling now as they dried. They evoked a scene from earlier that morning...Marta bringing a cup of tea to her. Lynn had not been ready to wake up, but she sat up anyway and accepted the gift. Yes, Marta had even put a little honey in the tea. They had sat side by side and sipped, Lynn trying to keep her eyes open. The sun had just begun peeping through the window. A ray lit up the crimson blossom of the geranium. Lynn couldn't remember the last time that plant had blossomed. And Marta had said, looking at it, "Now doesn't that say it all?"

Lynn had turned to check if she were joking. But Marta's eyes said she meant it. Lynn had sighed, knowing what she was about to say would not be welcome. "No. Actually it's not saying anything."

The spell was broken. "You mean like me?"

"Right."

Marta had gotten up and walked to the window.

79

Lynn said, "I'm sorry. I know you never made me any promises. It's just that that moment was so perfect. I want it to always be that way with us."

Marta had touched the red blossom. "This is the color of life. Its wondrous and delicate magnificence comes from nowhere. It is here a moment, like life, then it is gone—faded, drained away."

"The color of blood."

"You think of it as the color of evil, of anger, but for us it is joy. The red Goddess in her life aspect."

Now as Lynn stared at the geranium leaves, she thought, maybe there was some message there. The fragile basket seemed to pull apart as she looked. No words, but the pattern of the petals seemed familiar, then became a red blur as her eyes filled with tears. Now she was sure. Marta was gone again.

After a moment Lynn got angry. Self pity surely wouldn't help either of them. She really should throw the basket of leaves away before it became a fetish on her desk, one more thing to make her angry. It should take its place in the garbage of things to be recycled back into life. Isn't that what Marta would have said?

But the red pattern of petals haunted her. Had it been left as a warning? She felt something like the presence of an evil spirit that one must ward off with an offering. Marta had called it the color of life, but she couldn't shake the feeling that there was another more sinister meaning. Had she smelled something burnt?

Lynn went to wash the shreds of geranium leaves off her hands in the bathroom sink and realized that the prints were gone! Had Marta seen them and then been angry at Lynn, thinking that Lynn intended to use the pictures in an article? She went to look for the negatives. Her whole shoe box was gone!

Marta had promised to be here, had promised to tell Lynn what was going on. She had seemed so ready to ask for help. Why hadn't Lynn come home earlier?

Had the men from Asia Imports been here? But why would they take the pictures? Was there evidence that she had photographed by accident? She wished she had looked a little closer at the negatives. Now Lynn wondered if Marta's story had been a ruse to get at the photographs? Had Marta really intended to talk to the cops? Lynn looked in the desk drawer. The extra house key was there. But Marta might have gone out without taking it, knowing that Lynn was coming home first.

Then she remembered the contact sheets she had thrown away. She ran down into the basement. Thank god for incompetent management—the trash was still there in its unsavory pile of black and white plastic. She had tied hers with a pink rubber band. She found it and rummaged through quickly. The contacts and the extra prints were still there—just a little spaghetti sauce to rinse off. She carried them triumphantly back to her apartment to shoot negatives of them so she could enlarge them.

By eight-thirty Marta had still not come back. Lynn was sitting with a cup of coffee studying the pictures. She recognized two people off to one side of the stage when Marta was speaking. Dressed in jeans and T-shirts, the two 'importers' sat in second row seats on the outside aisle. Jason was leaning forward from the seat behind them, his arms around their shoulders. In another photo they were standing in the background by the stage. Jason was shaking hands with them as if they had just struck a deal.

She searched through her wallet for the card they had given her. She tried the phone number. There was not even an answering machine. She would have to check the address and pay them a visit tomorrow during office hours.

She curled up on the couch and fell asleep watching an old movie...and dreamed of the fierce black face of Kali with her necklace of skulls, her many arms and hands, all holding a cup of blood. She woke with a start. Marta had said that Kali was not evil, just powerful. "Evil as a thing in itself is part of the Western obsession with dichotomy." Remarkable how Marta's few words stuck with her.

It was after nine and still no Marta. For the first time Lynn was sure that Marta was mixed up in something illegal, even if she had not actually been the one to kill Sam. That had to be why she had been so silent and left so suddenly the first time. She didn't like the obvious conclusion—Marta had been deceiving her all along. But suddenly she envisioned Marta struggling, fighting to escape from the two 'importers'. Maybe they had hurt her, leaving blood on the rug that they had tried to wash out. Had Marta made the basket? A pile of petals they wouldn't notice? A cry for help?

Lynn dialed Del's number again and when she answered, blurted out, "Marta promised to be here tonight after the meeting. She was willing to talk to you about Sam and the murder, but she still hasn't come back yet."

"Great, now after she has disappeared again, you tell me she was going to give us some real information.... What the hell has happened to you. Suddenly your brains are in your—"

"She was on to something. Promised to tell me—make a statement for you. You were right; somebody searched my loft and took some negatives—photos I took at a Kalimaya meeting."

"It could be some of her cult buddies trying to keep their pictures out of the papers. Anything else taken?"

"No, but something was left—a little basket. Something Marta might leave, I suppose.... Maybe as a warning or a sign asking for help. I just don't know."

"Why didn't you get those pictures to us right away? We could have printed them in a safer place."

"I had no idea they might be of use to you. After she left the first time, I didn't want to have anything to do with them."

Del sighed. "You think she's in serious trouble?"

The image of Marta pale, bleeding, lying dead and forgotten.... Lynn took a deep breath. "Anyway, I fished some contacts I had thrown away out of the trash, reshot them and made enlargements. The two guys from Asia Imports were there in one of the photos. Looks like they might have been dealing, right there in the theater."

"Good girl. Sounds like you might have something. Call downtown, then get shots of your loft, of that basket. Tell them I told you to call. If anything develops call me right away. I'll meet you at my office in the morning."

At the station a sleepy desk sergeant's voice took her phone call. "Any evidence of a struggle?"

"There was a soapy wet spot on the rug. Like somebody had cleaned up. "

"Only the pictures gone?"

"As far as I can tell."

"Don't touch anything. Somebody'll be over."

It was Thomas who showed up with a couple of uniformed cops. Del and he always worked together. Lynn figured Del was still pissed at her. They got to work right away checking for fingerprints, testing the spot on the rug.

He took her statement. After she told her story, she asked, "Can you find Marta?"

He shrugged. "It's not like we haven't been trying to keep track of her all along. Nothing to go on here. Somebody did a real good job cleaning up. A professional job. No fingerprints. That tells us something, but there is no evidence leading to your girlfriend's whereabouts. Could have taken the negs and walked away. She walked out before."

"This time she was scared of somebody. She had found something out. She was planning to talk."

Thomas didn't hide his annoyance. "If that is true it's just too bad she waited. Why didn't you call us right away when she showed up again? We could have questioned her. We'd have something to go on."

Lynn could feel herself sinking into a helpless puddle.

Rog decided to show some compassion. "We'll do our best. We'll be looking for her anyway." Lynn gave him the blurry prints she had made, pointing out the two men who had come to the door.

He studied them for a while. "I'll check over my rogue's gallery. Something may click. Where are the new negs you shot?"

Lynn held up an envelope of negatives she had made from the contact prints. "I'll make more prints, then lock them up in the files at the office."

"When you're done with that come by my office and look at some mug shots for me."

• • •

When Lynn checked in at Del and Rog's office in the morning there was no news about Marta. She looked through Rog's gallery, but didn't match up anybody with her prints.

As far as she could tell, Del had forgiven her. Del told her, "Marta's cult buddies claimed they had no idea where she went after the meeting yesterday. They assumed she went to your house. Nobody seemed concerned. That fellow…. Singh is gone too. He left the meeting at the same time she did. Five o'clock. Seems strange they would have left before the end. Asia Imports seems to be legit—so far."

"She asked for my help; I don't believe she would have left without a word, a note, something. She promised."

Del's annoyance showed again. "Didn't it occur to you that she might be lying to you and never intended to talk to us?"

Now it was Lynn's turn to be mad, both at Del and at Marta. …And at herself. She had let Del down. Now she felt it was her responsibility to find out what the hell was going on.

Rog said more sympathetically, "We couldn't get anybody at the Society offices to tell us what the meeting was about, let alone what decisions were made. But we'll keep on it. We will find her one way or another. "

• • •

Lynn called Asia Imports during office hours and the woman who answered the phone said that no one could talk to her at the moment, everyone was out of town.

She found the office down by the river in the warehouse district. Seedy storefronts, faded signs—a walk up address. The name was freshly painted on the front door, Asia Imports Inc., Allen and Gruber underneath, but the door was locked.

She called what had to be an answering service from the phone booth on the corner. This time she insisted on making an appointment with somebody. Told the woman that the man whose name was on the card, George Allen, had promised to see her. The woman reluctantly made an appointment for three in the afternoon.

She sat in her car watching the building until Blue Suit showed up. She waited a few minutes after the man she assumed was George Allen entered the building and then followed him in. The door was unlocked this time. The room was cool and slightly musty. There was a receptionist's desk, the chair pushed back as if someone had just left. Art works from various places in Asia were rather haphazardly placed around the small office. A stuffed parrot and animal pelts were in a glass case. Was it still legal to import those? In a tiny inner office, she saw Blue Suit, his coat casually draped across the back of his chair, his tie loose, papers strewn across his desk.

He stood up smiling, his hand out. "George Allen here. Good to see you again. What can we do for you?"

She touched his hand briefly and tried to sit down casually in the chair across from him, her heart thumping. "I'm thinking of traveling in Asia, visiting my friend Marta Handley there. You remember; you said when you came to my door that you were interested in having her work with you. I thought I would get more information from you about what that would involve."

He sat down and leaned back. She couldn't read the expression on his face, but somehow it didn't make her feel secure. "Sorry we barged in on you like that. Someone told us she was there and we were anxious to talk to her. So she did get in touch with you after all?" Was it a statement or a question?

She nodded, feeling as if he could read her face.

He dropped the front legs of his chair to the floor and leaned toward her. "I really would rather talk with her directly. If you could just tell me where to find her."

He seemed genuinely not to know where Marta was. Lynn felt almost relieved; perhaps he wasn't responsible for Marta's disappearance. "She would rather you dealt with me. If you just give me the information."

He shuffled his papers as if looking for something in particular, then said, "There are some things she could help us with." He added some incomprehensible comments about trade relations and import duties. "Perhaps we could all meet." He touched her hand. "How about dinner, on us of course."

"Marta isn't in the country at the moment. That's why I'm here."

He drummed his fingers on the desk top and stared at her suspiciously. "I happen to know she was at a meeting just yesterday."

How did he know that? "Are you a member of the Kalimaya's then? Were you at that meeting?"

He looked at her for a moment, leaning back in his chair and pulling apart a paper clip. Then he shook his head slowly. He put a pad of paper in front of her. "Just give us her address in Nepal. We can contact her there."

"She wants me to be her agent in dealing with such matters."

"Shall we send material for her to your apartment then?"

Lynn nodded and stood up.

He held out a pamphlet to her. "When you see her give her this."

"I'll let her know what you said." She left the building as mystified as when she came.

She called Del.

Del met her at her apartment with pizza and beer. "Look, he isn't going to blow his cover for your convenience. Eat your pizza. I'll see what I can find out about Gruber and Allen."

"You said they are legitimate."

"Yeah, they do have all the proper paperwork done. But they've only been in business for a short time. I suspect if we dig deep enough we'll find something."

• • •

When Lynn called Asia Imports again the next morning, she got a recorded message saying that Mr. Allen was out of town for a few days.

She called Peter O'Hara at his office. He didn't have anything about Asia Imports, but he was interested that they might be pressuring the Kalimaya Society to set up some sort of trade deal from Nepal. "It could be a legitimate import scheme. People do it all the time. But it would make a good cover for a drug operation."

"But why the Kalimaya?"

"A lot of Kalimaya devotees are making the trip to the new retreat there. I talked to an ex-convert the other day about the place. He had a great time. There were no drugs available at the retreat itself, but outside a little money went a long way. And someone who was a Kalimaya member approached him to smuggle stuff into the U.S. Not anybody in the leadership per se. He also said it was just a glorified tourist resort. Just the type of tourist that wouldn't make Customs suspicious."

"There was a meeting of the Society leadership yesterday. I understand an important decision was made about fund raising, maybe illegal fund raising. A Kalimaya member, Marta Handley, disappeared from my apartment just before telling me what she knew about that meeting. I don't think she went will-

86

ingly. And someone stole photos and negatives that I took at the meeting the night I met you. Fortunately I had dumped a contact print in the garbage."

"Marta—wasn't she a suspect in the Sam Jenson case?"

"Right."

"Interesting. I would like a look at those photos. Come by and we'll check them off against some in my files."

• • •

On her way to Peter's office, Lynn went to the house where Marta had been living when they first met. The rooms were empty and there was a 'for lease' sign in the window. When she found the landlord, he said, "That religious lot left still owing me rent. Should never have rented to them." He let her look around. The place was clean, all the posters and notices gone. She found some phone numbers written on the wall next to the phone.

The landlord said, defensively, "Can't afford to paint these places every time I have new renters. You've no idea the expense of keeping up these old houses. Wood rots, people don't take care of things anymore. Had to repaint the living room—one corner was covered with red powder and sticky food. Disgusting."

Lynn remembered the Kali altar. She wondered where the little girl was making her drawings now. She picked up a rather slick brochure from one of the cupboards. The picture of the Victorian mansion she had seen on their bulletin board was on the front.

The landlord was saying, "Surprisingly, that bunch actually had good references. Just goes to show."

"Who recommended them?"

He gave her an out—of—state phone number. "Respectable people. Been in the hotel business for years. I guess sometimes even they go off the deep end."

Later when Lynn called the number and asked about the Kalimaya's and about Marta, a woman asked rudely, "Why do you want to know?"

Lynn tried to guess which tack to take. Was this woman a Kalimaya defector, or would she try to protect them? "I'm trying to locate my sister. She...."

"Why don't you try the operator. The Society has several

offices nationwide." The phone slammed down.

• • •

Peter O'Hara's office looked as if the Mafia had just ran-
sacked it. Papers and books everywhere. He was squatting in
front of a large filing cabinet when she came in. He handed her a
stack of papers. "Take a look at these."

Lynn lifted a pile of books off the only chair and put them
carefully on the floor, the only available space. He had given her
a stack of letters from Kalimaya defectors. Peter explained that
they had been in response to the series of editorials he had written when the Kalimayas had first appeared in Hartfield. "I just
gave you the ones that have stuff in them that might be relevant."

Lynn read through them carefully while Peter looked at the
photos. Then she handed them back impatiently. "Just a lot of
rumors about illegal deals and devil worship by people who
needed reasons to leave the fold. There's nothing that relates to
Marta, or Sam's murder for that matter."

"To be trite, where there is smoke there's usually fire. I
haven't had the time to interview many of them. That would be
the next step." He shook his head and handed Lynn back the
photos. "I don't see anything new here. I haven't a clue why
someone would want to take them."

Lynn sighed. "If I could just talk to Marta. I know she was on
to something. But even if they know where she is, her cult buddies won't tell me."

Peter shrugged. "It's usually when you're ready to give up
that the inspiration comes. Kalimaya files are second drawer
down. Feel free to browse. Just remember you owe me on this
one. I have a hunch you will find her and her information, otherwise I wouldn't gamble with five years worth of files. He pulled
open the drawer and went back to his desk.

After she left his office with a few xeroxed sheets that
seemed relevant she went down to the mission. Maybe somebody
there would talk to her. There were no clients today. Workmen
were tearing out a brick wall. The noise was deafening.

Nancy was alone in her office. This time her eyes narrowed
when she saw Lynn. She had to raise her voice almost to a shout
to be heard over the bedlam behind her. "I know who you're looking for; she isn't working here any more. The traitor abandoned

her mission with us like I said she would. If you ask me, all her spiritual superiority was just an excuse for getting out of work anyway. Now she cares more about those Nepal people than she ever did about us."

A woman carrying a bag of food stopped on her way to the kitchen to say, "I don't think you should say those things about Marta. She's always been devoted to the work of the Kalimayas."

Nancy said angrily to the woman, "Then why was she studying Nepalese language? And why did she have to go there all the time? If she is so devoted to our work, why isn't she here now, helping us like she said she would?"

The woman walked away without saying any more.

Lynn turned back to Nancy. "Is Marta in Nepal now? Do you know where Marta is?"

"I don't know and I don't really care anymore."

"Would you mind if I looked at her office?"

"The police have already been through it. What they didn't take I threw out. It's going to be my office."

Lynn smiled. "It looks as if the mission is doing well if you can do all this construction."

"We've managed to do some fund-raising even without Marta's help."

Lynn remembered that Marta had talked about wanting to buy the warehouse next door to turn it into a homeless shelter. She asked about the construction going on. She was told the Kalimayas had bought the next building and were constructing a passageway between the two. It was to be a meditation hall. So much for Marta's shelter. But Lynn did wonder where had they gotten the money for such a project?

"What you're doing here is very interesting. Congratulations. You must have found some very generous donors."

Nancy frowned. "I'm very busy today."

" Do you mind if I interview some people here?"

Nancy shrugged and Lynn followed the woman into the kitchen. Maybe she would have something helpful to say. At least she seemed more sympathetic.

The woman was chopping vegetables. Lynn sat down next to her and explained that she needed to get in contact with Marta.

"As far as we know here, she is still at the retreat in Nepal.

She was here for the big policy meeting of course, but she went right back there." She leaned closer and whispered, "Rumor has it that she has left the Kalimayas to work helping the local people in Nepal. She's been trying to get the Society to fund some projects there for a long time. You know the life expectancy there is not much more than forty years—worse for women. Infant mortality is terrible, the land is being eroded away at a terrible rate. Nobody in the Kalimayas wants to think about that. It spoils the image. How could they get rich Americans to pay a lot of money to go to their spiritual retreat if that kind of information got out? They are too busy being spiritual."

"So you think Marta really is back in Nepal?"

The woman shrugged. "That's the story they gave out to us, although I personally doubt she would be meditating like they say. I don't know why she would go back there again. She told me last time I saw her that the contradictions between the way foreigners can live their lives and the life of the local people were too much for her. After all, her mother was from there." She leaned closer. "Nancy thinks that Marta has left the Kalimaya Society altogether. But I don't believe she would abandon us."

Lynn went next to Mr. Singh's plush offices. The secretary claimed everyone was out of town. She took Lynn's name and promised that Mr. Singh or one of his assistants would call her when they were available.

On the way back to her office, Lynn passed the old movie theater on Market street. A local theater group was rehearsing Hamlet so the door was open. There was no one in the lobby and she could hear the dramatic tones of the actors from the stage. A poster of the eight-armed Kali was still up, with some notices stapled over her. Lynn took the poster.

Back in her office, she stuck Kali on the wall and sat staring at the image with that unpleasant person in the back of her head saying, *Why don't you burn some incense too? Maybe she'll materialize out of the ether.*

She called some Kalimaya offices in other cities with no better results. Then she picked up the slick brochure. The address wasn't local—somewhere up in the mountains in a resort area. When she called, a man answered, his foreign voice impatient. She asked for Marta.

"Marta, there is no Marta here."

Lynn said hastily before he could hang up. "Can you tell me where she's gone?"

A woman came on the line, a local voice with the ring of false politeness. "Who is calling please?"

"I'm a friend of Marta Handley. Did she leave an address where she can be reached?"

Lynn could imagine the stretch of the smile across face. It pinched the words that came over the phone. "I am sorry. That information is confidential. Please give me your name."

"That information is confidential." Lynn slammed down the phone, then regretted it immediately. Not the way a good investigative reporter works. She knew how to bludgeon verbally well enough to get information out of bureaucrats. But it was best to do it face to face.

Bill was at the window watering his plants. He picked up the brochure. "Why don't you go on up there? It's not that far away."

"Marta probably was sent off with the Kalimaya evangelists to Newport or parts unknown to recruit."

Bill sat down to admire his greenery."But the people up there at this retreat would likely know where she is. It's not that big an organization."

"The people at the mission didn't know."

"Didn't know or wouldn't tell."

"What reason had they to hide Marta's whereabouts?"

"You got the police looking for her again. Even more reason for the Society to cover her tracks."

"They're no more likely to talk to me."

"Tell them you're looking for an old roommate. She left stuff and unpaid bills behind. You say you're worried about her. You know how to wear people down until they tell you what you want to know. You do it all the time. Anyway they'll think you just want your money and once you get that, they are rid of you." He shrugged. "Probably happens with those itinerant religious types all the time. And it wouldn't hurt to look recruitable. Like you've got some extra money to play with. They'll take you in with open arms. Just hope that your friend hasn't talked too much about you being a reporter."

"If she left voluntarily."

"If they're that afraid of the press then, you can bet, they've got something to hide."

"Marta said they hate reporters because the press has treated them like something between a circus and a vaudeville show. She takes her faith seriously."

"It takes some true believers to make any scam work. If she is naive enough to be taken in by a double dealer in her organization, she might even have given away the fact that she was thinking about talking to the police."

Lynn's heart caught in her throat. Marta was not naive, but she trusted people. It was just the kind of person she was. Not that she was not intelligent enough to know better. It was a deliberate choice to trust a person's best motives. She might very well have told someone she felt obligated to go to the police if the the members of the Kalimaya Society didn't agree not to indulge in illegal fund raising. Of course they would try to get rid of her.

But maybe it was she, Lynn, who was the naive one. She was the trusting one, believing in Marta's sincerity, an easy mark for a clever scheming woman. It had all been an act. She looked the other way to hide the tears. She had to find Marta. She had to know if the woman had been lying to her, had used her...or...if there was really something still between them.

9

For the six hour drive, much of it along wooded rural roads, Marta's face haunted the shadows of Lynn's thoughts. Finally Lynn reached the turnoff, based on directions from the pamphlet. Two miles over rolling hills and she saw the house, a huge Victorian, built when materials and labor were still cheap, when so many craftsmen were immigrating from Europe, and the newly rich could afford to imitate the English minor gentry. She tried to ask questions about the place in the local grocery store, but all anyone would say was that it belonged to some spiritual group.

As Lynn drove up to the house, she imagined a time when ladies in long gowns played croquet on the lawn. The flowering bushes that must once have been carefully trimmed had gone wild, taking over much of the grounds. Still, it looked more like a country club than an ashram.

What she did see, beyond the cut lawns, were people in white uniforms playing tennis and jogging down the rose-lined paths.

She went up the broad granite steps into a high-ceilinged front hall with a marble floor. There was an ornate table with attached mirror, coat rack and umbrella stand that might very well have been put there when the house was built. Incongruously, next to it was the modern desk and filing cabinet for the receptionist. Lynn could imagine the architect who had designed the house gagging at the tastelessness.

The receptionist, a pale young man with long dark locks, who looked skinny enough to have been on a rice diet for months, was on the phone. On a cork announcement board, lists of workshops were neatly posted. When the receptionist put down the phone Lynn said matter-of-factly, "Where is the listing of workshop rooms. I don't remember...."

The receptionist smiled at her, saying almost too sweetly, "Are you a Scorpio or a Leo?"

Lynn tried to look innocent. "A Leo. Can't you tell by my golden mane?"

The young man looked confused. "Leo's are meeting in the red room down the hall to your left. Third door." He eyed Lynn's gray tweed jacket and shoulder bag. "You can change in the dressing room next door." He pointed with long skinny fingers, pale to the tips—all he needed was a good hearty meal or two and some sunshine, she thought, and he might actually start looking good.

She headed down the hall, waiting in the dressing room until its one occupant left, and then commandeered a white suit of soft cotton out of the clothes hamper in the corner.

The red room was indeed red. Lovely shades of rose shading to red-purple. What good taste to have left the original wallpaper. She took a pillow and settled down on the big oriental rug with the handful of others waiting there. Their glances did not welcome her; they seemed too self-absorbed for that. And these are supposed to be fellow Leo's?—Lynn could only be amused.

After a while, a young man came into the room. Dressed in a formal white suit that emphasized the handsome mahogany of his complexion, he was tall for an Indian with a narrow body and eyes that seemed too large for his face. He sat down on a pillow facing them, careful to arrange the creases in his trousers, then pressed his palms together in the Indian fashion and greeted them bowing his head and smiling. The "audience" returned the gesture that Lynn did her best to mimic. She could feel the leader's eyes fasten on her for a second, his lashes blinking quickly. Then he smiled. She tried to smile back but her nervousness must have showed.

"Did the Sister send you?"

"Marta told me I should come."

In an annoyed tone the woman next to her said, "The introductory sessions are on Thursday. Didn't she tell you?"

The Indian said, "You take her down to the office, Jane." He said to Lynn. "They will explain our procedure to you—get you enrolled if need be." He stood and came over to Lynn reaching out to help her stand, and touched her back too intimately as he ushered her to the door. His whisper and eyes were blatantly seductive. "I'm sure I will see you again soon. Welcome to our family."

Jane, leading her down the hall, knocked on a door and, when there was an answer, pushed her inside, calling out before she hurried away, "A new one; you need to explain the proper procedures to her."

Behind the desk sat none other than Jason, the juggler, his blond hair cut short now, making him look more boyish. He hadn't looked up at her entrance and Lynn debated whether to cut and run. But what did she have to lose? At worst, he just wouldn't tell her where Marta was. At least he couldn't pretend he didn't know Marta.

When he finally looked up she said, "There was just a little confusion. Your receptionist thought I was a member of the Leo group. I came looking for Marta—since she left so suddenly, and I still have a few of her belongings, some mail. I'm a little worried about her."

Jason swiveled around in his chair and looked at her for a long moment as if debating what to do. It was almost as if he had expected her. He stood up, and held out his hand. He too was dressed in a fashionable white suit, but it looked a bit more rumpled on his large frame. "I'm Jason Goodrich." Was he going to pretend they had never met? When they shook hands, Lynn could feel his nervousness in the dampness of his palm. He continued, "Marta Handley is on a retreat."

"When do you expect her back?"

"I'm sure she will contact you when she returns, if she is concerned about her things, or you can give them to me." He smiled disarmingly. "I'll see that they are kept safe for her. I'm surprised she didn't explain it all to you before she left." He came around the desk and reached for her elbow as if to usher her out.

Lynn stood her ground. "I would like an address where she can be reached."

"I'm sorry but that information—"

She finished his sentence for him. "—is confidential. I'm sorry, too, but I have reason to believe that Marta may be in danger."

"I'm surprised she didn't leave you a note. She left some time ago. Why did you wait so long to look for her if you thought there was something wrong?"

Was he lying or didn't he know that she had been back to Lynn's so recently? "Some men came looking for her, and then my apartment was searched."

"What did the men look like?"

"They said they were from Asia Imports." Feeling that this might be the last person she should show it to, she hesitantly took out the card and handed it to him.

He glanced at the card and tapped it impatiently against his other hand. Looking at her as if she were a school child who had forgotten her homework, he said, "I do believe there are two of our religious family that work for this company."

The feeling that Marta was in danger came back more strongly. "Then why didn't they know where she was? Why didn't they ask you where she was instead of me? Is Marta—are your members regularly in the business of importing?"

He frowned. "Our members are free agents. A little legal trading during their travels is not frowned upon."

He was avoiding her questions. Time to be more straight forward. "The police are looking for Marta. They agree with me that her last disappearance was mysterious. After coming here, I'm still not satisfied...."

"Yes, the police have made inquiries. I assure you she is quite safe. Marta is in Nepal on retreat."

"In that case. I would like her address there."

Jason moved toward the door. "We can not reveal that information. You will have to wait until she contacts you."

"I am not moving until you tell me how to get in touch with her."

Jason sighed. "Maybe there is someone that you will believe." He took her arm. "Come with me." She reluctantly went with him. He knocked gently on another door. A distinctive, melodious woman's voice called out quietly. "Come in, certainly."

He opened the door and they stepped into a darkened room. Jason stuttered an apology. "Sorry to interrupt, but this seemed important."

In the murky room Lynn didn't recognize the Indian woman

at first, her gray hair pulled back in a bun. "It is always something important. You Americans cannot imagine that something could be done on another day or in another hour when one is prepared. No, no, come in. Who is this you have with you? Yes, I know you. You are our little Marta's friend."

By the voice Lynn knew this to be the woman they called The Sister. But she didn't remember her being so small; she barely came up to Lynn's shoulder. Was this the same woman who had seemed so powerful at the meeting?

The woman shooed Jason toward the door. "Go on. Attend to your tasks." He handed her the Asia Imports card without a word and left the room.

The Sister took Lynn's hand and led her over to soft silken pillows piled around a low table. "You will have a little tea with me and then you can tell me what this is all about." She poured out two cups and Lynn sat down in front of one of them, feeling soothed by the Sister's presence.

"Darjeeling tea. It's one thing the British did well—organize the tea gardens." The Sister went to a lamp, took out a pair of round spectacles, and examined the card. Then she sighed and looked at Lynn. "Our Marta was impatient for answers too. She did not understand that things have their own time. She wanted so badly to make things right."

"Why do you speak of her in the past tense."

The woman smiled and nodded. "You have a good ear. Our dear little sister is continuing her mission elsewhere, taking time out for a retreat. Our demands on her have made her weary, and, of course, our Marta always tries to reach out to so many. She gathers the troubled around her. Like many who want to help, she does not see the necessity for some boundaries in this life. She tries to do too much. And she asks too much of those around her. She has been given permission for an extended meditation, to focus on the inner discipline. She is not to be disturbed with worldly matters." She patted Lynn's hand.

How calming was this nice, refined lady with her gentle wisdom, surely from an upper Indian caste, well educated, elegant, though dressed in the simple cotton sari. Maybe Lynn's imagination had been getting away from her. There was no evidence that these people weren't exactly what they seemed to be. Perhaps Marta had been right to be wary of her as a reporter—it was easy to suspect religious groups of being criminal after some of the recent scandals.

But Lynn had a feeling this woman knew more than she was saying. Was she really the kind, like Marta, who always believed in people's better side and tended not to notice when they were being taken in by swindlers and cheats?

And should she mention the meeting of the Society that Marta had just attended? Surely the woman knew about that. "I thought I heard that she was at a recent Society meeting. I must have been mistaken."

The woman smiled confidently. "Even were she here, she would not be burdened with administrative details. "

So the Sister was not at the meeting. "I am glad to know where Marta is and that she is all right. I would like to be able to write to her. Surely you can give me her address."

The Sister smiled. "If you like, you can write a note and we will get it to her."

"I wouldn't want to trouble you. An address...."

The woman sighed. She took Lynn's hands again and squeezed them warmly. "I am sorry, my dear. I can see that you care for her. True caring is a rare gift. She knew you would come checking. I must tell you that she asked us not to tell you where she is."

Lynn pulled her hands away. Could it be true that Marta didn't want to see her? She turned for a moment to think, away from this woman's spell. There was still the murder under investigation, and Marta had come back. She had said she needed help. She had had something to tell Lynn. And she had promised not to leave again without an explanation. And who was it that had taken the negatives and searched her loft? If it was Marta, Lynn needed to know why.

The Sister offered no comment about the phony import company. If they weren't involved in something illegal, why had Jason been worried enough to bring her to the Sister?

Lynn held out her hand for the business card. "I'd appreciate it if you could tell me what you know about this company. I intend to investigate them further. Why were they looking for Marta?"

The Sister placed the business card on the table in front of Lynn, and held her cup of tea between her palms for a moment, her eyes closed. Her body seemed to radiate a sadness. Then her eyes opened slowly, and her face was quiet and calm again. Her beautiful ringed fingers formed a lotus shape. "A flower cannot exist in its splendor without a stem and roots that reach out into the earth with its rotting soil and creeping vermin, and cleansing water. Perhaps you, with your Western thinking, can't see Lahkshmi in the Lotus flower because you are looking for a worm." She smiled. "And then isn't a worm or an an insect, a beautiful thing too?"

"Flowers are killed by insects. We Westerners tend to think we can kill off the worms and save the flowers. And most of us do prefer flowers over worms if given the choice."

The Sister smiled sadly. "Perhaps it would help if I read you a passage from one of Marta's letters. Then you might understand a little better."

The Sister went to a low cabinet, shuffled through some papers and came back with a piece of blue stationary to read:

Dear Sister;

I have meditated today at the lake that is the Mother of us all. I can not express the joyful spirituality of this place. I feel at once renewed and fulfilled. Filled with Kali-maya.

Here I am away from the filth of plastic, metal, and putrid gasses they create to kill us—Here there are mountains and woods and people with smooth faces because they touch the Earth everyday. Thank you for sending me here.

It's too bad they must still burn wood to cook with. It makes breathing difficult sometimes in the valleys...."

The Sister smiled at Lynn. "Well, enough for you to see that she wants to be where she is."

"May I see the letter?"

She reluctantly handed the blue sheet to Lynn. There was no date and no address and it was clearly only one of several pages. Lynn read the rest of the page:

It is too bad there are so many people for such a fragile land, so much erosion in spite of their conservative terracing. One cannot help but wish the Indian farmers who have immigrated to Nepal would....

The page ended. Lynn turned it; nothing on the other side.

"May I read the rest?"

Lynn could see from the Sister's expression that she had overstepped the bounds of politeness. Hastily Lynn said, "I appreciate your sharing the letter."

Should she tell the Sister that she had seen Marta so recently? After all this woman was Marta's spiritual mother. Surely Marta would have been in contact when she came back from Nepal—if indeed that was where she had been. Unless there was something seriously wrong.

Lynn decided to take a chance in the hope of more information. She watched the Sister's face carefully as she told her, "But I saw her. Just days ago in Hartfield—"

The Sister reacted with a startled, puzzled look. Then she put her hand over Lynn's comfortingly. "Dreams can be very real. She did visit you. She has a very strong spirit, and I know she does care for you."

Lynn was annoyed. "No, I mean she was there physically, in my apartment. I'm pretty sure she was in some sort of trouble. She said she would meet me last night to explain, but she never showed and someone searched my apartment. A strange basket of leaves was left too. I think Marta left it as a sign, a call for help."

The Sister's eyes sparked with annoyance in the dim light at the mention of the basket. Her voice grew strong and sharp. "Marta is in Nepal. I know this—she is my spiritual daughter. She would do nothing without consulting me first. You must not use such subterfuge. Tell me what it is you want from me. I will not tolerate such lies."

"I am not lying. I—"

The Sister turned away. "Marta is not in this country. There was no reason for her to come back. I have other letters from her. You are mistaken."

"In that case, give me an address so I can get in touch with her to prove to myself she's safe."

There was still an edge to the Sister's voice. "It is late, and there is still much for me to do. Like every family, ours requires a good deal of care...."

Lynn said, "I'm sorry I've upset you. It's just that I am so concerned about her...just give me an address so I can feel reassured. It's not that I don't believe you. It's just...."

Lynn was relieved that the Sister didn't try to dismiss her, but put her palms together slowly and deliberately touching the tips of her fingers to her upper lip against the edges of her nostrils to breath slowly for what seemed to Lynn like an eternity.

Lynn gradually felt the energy around her change. She sighed and closed her own eyes to feel a lightness flow through her. For a moment it seemed as if none of this mattered, only the flow of images across her eyelids.

The Sister's voice—low and gentle. "Stay with us for the night, and tomorrow, if you like, write a note to our dear Marta and we will see that she gets it. Talk with our members, our guests. You will be able to judge for yourself the meaning and purpose of our organization. Whatever evil threatens is not here. It can not touch us unless we let it."

Lynn's eyes fluttered open. The Sister's placid eyes drew her in, warm and friendly once again. "Marta knows that. She has the Goddess in her. Dream of her here and you will know what she knows."

Was the woman trying to hypnotize her? Again she was fearful. She shook off the magic. This woman was the Kalimaya's leader. There had to be a reason why she wouldn't let Lynn see more of the letter. How could she not know if they were 'fundraising' with illegal drug money? Was she inviting Lynn to stay so she, too, could disappear?

Her practical side scoffed, told her she was seeing bad guys everywhere. The woman before her was, like Marta, a sincere, if naive, religious leader. She should be glad for an overnight stay. That would give her the chance she needed to look around. She smiled at the woman. "Thank you. My boss knows I'm here and it's a long way back. I would like to do that."

The Sister rang a little bell and another Indian woman dressed in a sari came in. The Sister said something to her in what must have been Hindi. She led Lynn to a small room without windows. Lynn hesitated. It looked too much like a cell. But she was relieved to see that there was no lock on the door; the old keyhole was filled with plastic wood. The woman saw her look at it and said, "The Sister says locks are the worldly expression of mistrust."

There was a neat white blanketed cot, a towel on a wall rack, a small table with a bowl of fruit, a thermos and cup. On the wall above the table was a picture of the Sister surrounded by young men in white.

The woman said, "The thermos has hot tea, there is more in the kitchen."

"Where is everyone?"

"At evening meditation. Some people like to walk before they sleep. We have a lounge in the roof garden. Feel free to look at our library just down the hall. We encourage people to go to sleep by ten. Breakfast is early. Some of us are in the habit of rising with the sun." She smiled apologetically. "It comes from living in the tropics where the early morning is best for working because it is still cool."

After the woman left, Lynn sat on the cot, suddenly very tired. She looked around, observing that the narrow room had once been part of a larger room which had been divided into several such white, wood-panelled cells.

She got her day pack with a change of clothes and her toothbrush from the car. Would she lie awake all night wondering who might wander through that door?

Still, the lack of locks would make her snooping easier. Marta was in danger and the Sister might not be so virtuous and wise as she appeared. She'd said that one must accept the roots and vermin as well as the flower—another way of saying that drug trade was necessary for financing their work?

Lynn walked around the house, found the meditation hall with its rows of silent people. There were some locked doors. Jason's office had a lock. There was no light coming from under the door, so she tried the knob, her heart pounding. Locked. Lynn knew she had to see the rest of Marta's letters, so she headed to the room where she had met the Sister. But there was a light under the door.

Frustrated, she went into the deserted library and looked through a dog-eared copy of the Bhagavad-Gita in English with pictures. Soon, bored with that, she studied a thin paperback written by the Sister entitled *Mahishsuramardini as Spiritual Energy*.

At about 9 o'clock, she returned to her room, purposely

102

leaving her door ajar to watch people wandering down the hallway. At ten, the hall lights dimmed. At ten-thirty Lynn took her toothbrush, soap and towel as cover for her search, and went down the hall, ostensibly to look for a shower room.

She stood once again outside the door where she had talked with the Sister. No light shone underneath. She opened the door quickly and slipped inside turning on a little flashlight she had brought from her car. The room was empty. She went quickly to the cabinet. It was locked with a padlock. So much for the woman's trust. The cabinet was old, the doors loose. With her pocket knife she loosened the wood screws holding the latch onto the doors. Inside she found several of the blue pieces of paper, all letters from Marta.

She put them in order by the dates and read them quickly, They had been written just before Sam's death. Marta had been in Nepal earlier in the spring. Lynn noted that the letter the Sister had read to her had been written in April. So the Sister had lied, tried to make Lynn believe the letters had come recently. What else had she lied about?

3/ May—I've had no success convincing Raj that the importers should be excluded from our presence. I don't know what to do. Send me some instructions. They are more entrenched in their path than we had suspected.

9/ May—I suggested to Raj that we start a fund for tuberculosis treatment. He said that they were Buddhists and had their own path to enlightenment considering themselves to be born and to die in the shadow of Durga's sacred mountains. He has such a beatific smile it is hard to discuss anything with him. I wish you were here with all your wisdom. I know you are needed there, but if you were here everyone would do what you say without argument. Even though I am your messenger, no one seems to hear what I say.

20/May—Strangers have arrived and are being treated royally. Raj won't answer any of my questions. Forgive me. I am finding it hard to stay on the path and let my doubt and my fear pass through me. I fear he has not let go of his attachment to the material plane.

The greed of some of these men—their obvious contempt for the local people—I am afraid, truly. They spend like thieves. Raj says we can't afford to question the sources of our revenue. The retreat and its work are too important. I don't know what to do.

Raj sent me on a pilgrimage, to meditate in the mountains.

3/May—I went to my mother's village even though you advised me not to. I felt compelled to do it, though now I see you were right. It upset me terribly. Her people are very poor. They are the Tamang, what the Hindus call a caste here, although they are more a truly different culture than a caste. I remembered some of the words Mother taught me, and am learning more. I want to find some way to help them. They are my people, after all.

10/ May—Forgive me for veering from the path. You set me a task, but the material plane is too strong. Meditation today was impossible. My cousin has tuberculosis, and can't stop coughing.

Now I know why I see such smooth faces. So few old people. They die here so young. Finally Raj did let me use some money to send my cousin to the city for treatment.

I must confess to you my fear of Raj. Fasting and meditation have not dispelled my reservation at the involvement of the men who would have us participate in their importing venture.

Lynn held the crinkled pieces of paper next to her cheek. Smelled the faint scent of sandalwood. Did she dare take them, even to copy them? She regretted that she didn't have a photographic memory.

She looked quickly through the other compartments in the desk hoping for something more recent. Nothing but personal correspondence, most of it in a language she couldn't read.

Jackpot—there were several Asia Imports receipts listing items bought by Allen and his partner Gruber; figurines, jewelry, paid for with an exorbitant amount of money. Not really proof of anything illegal...yet.

If she stole Marta's letters and the receipts she would have to leave at once. It would be better to stay the night and look around in the morning as if she were really interested in being converted. Maybe she could talk her way into staying longer. There was a lot more to find out.

She replaced everything as closely as she could to the way she had found it, and put the screws back. There was nothing else in the room except the table, the pillow and curtained windows. There was a little trash basket next to the desk. She looked through it and came up with the ultimate treasure, a blue envelope with Marta's name and address in Nepal, postmarked July.

There was a noise in the hallway. Lynn shut off her flashlight and went to the door. Nothing. She opened it a crack and looked out. There was a whiff of soapy cologne in the air. She slipped out and headed for the bathroom, her towel over her shoulder.

She nearly ran into Jason, still damp from a shower, dressed only in a short terry cloth robe that barely covered his thighs. He blocked her way. "What are you doing here? I thought we got rid of you once and for all."

Lynn could smell whiskey on his breath. She tried to move on past him. "The Sister invited me to stay the night."

Jason frowned menacingly, drops of moisture glistening on his handsome tanned face "And why are you wandering the halls after everyone else is asleep?"

She murmured about how she wasn't used to going to sleep so early and tried to push past him. He didn't move.

Lynn stood back, her arms folded, trying to get some distance. "If you really want to get rid of me, the best way would be to give me a clue where Marta might be."

"Not here, that's for sure. The Sister told you. Marta's in Nepal. Hiding out in the hills. Meditating, getting her head together. So she will come back and be her old hardworking, submissive self. And she does not want to see or hear from you. Now why don't you just go home like a good girl."

Lynn tried to look cool, leaned against the wall to wait for him to get out of her way. "Thanks for the advice. I'll try to keep it in mind. Let's hope those Immigration people don't get her on her way back into the country."

He looked a little puzzled. "She was born here, no passport troubles that I know of." He frowned. "Unless she was lying to me." He moved closer. "What Immigration people?"

"The ones who came to the door pretending that they were

importers. I showed you the card."

His eyes narrowed. "They weren't from Immigration. What're you trying to pull?"

"They told me they were. Of course, maybe you know more about them than I do. Aren't they your new funding source?"

He looked a little startled then said, "You don't know anything. You're just looking for trouble. If that's what you want, we can provide it for you." Lynn began moving slowly around him, feeling like she had as a child trying to get to the grocery store past the drunk on the corner who liked to do a little friendly teasing, and past the empty store-front where sometimes a man would hide to expose himself to the kids on the block. Somehow he was never there when the grown-ups were with her. And where were all the grown-ups now?

The smell of alcohol overwhelmed even the strong cologne as he grabbed her arm and tightened his grip. He leaned close to whisper threateningly in her ear, "You may be able to fool the Sister, but I know why you're here. You're not looking for Marta; you're trying to dig up dirt to smear us in the Press. Marta was just a way to get at us."

Lynn pulled away from him. "If you have nothing to hide why not let me look around. Why are you afraid to let me talk to Marta? Your guru lady invited me to stay. She isn't worried about what I might write. She showed me some of Marta's letters."

He folded his arms across his chest, a smug look on his face. "Marta isn't here. You might as well leave." When Lynn didn't retreat he continued. "You know Marta wasn't ever really interested in you. She had a little karmic burn-out, that's all. Your apartment was just convenient. Gave her space—and a place to meet her drop-outs, her greasy street people. She's been my old lady for years. You were just a momentary lapse."

He gave her a brotherly jab to the shoulder. "Nice looking chick like you, I can see why you turn her on."

She reminded herself this was a relatively public place and the attempted intimacy was just another form of intimidation to get her to leave.

She tried again to get by him and he danced to block her way like a boxer in the ring. "Come on, a pretty lady like you shouldn't waste her time chasing after a cold fish like Marta-doll. She's only got the hots for the spiritual. Can't be bothered with us fleshed-out mortals." He giggled. "I know all the tricks, kid. Let me show you a little flesh before we...get rid of you."

Suddenly he grabbed her and lifted her off the floor, his hand across her mouth. She felt herself being carried by this tide of human muscle, like a fish in a net. She saw the door to his office ahead and began to struggle in panic.

Jason laughed as he fumbled for the knob. She thought in amazement, the man really seemed to think he could get away with it. Now it was time to try and yell. She took a deep breath, but all that came out was an awkward squeak. Before she could try again, Jason dropped her at the feet of the Sister, who stood looking down at her through her reading glasses as if she were an interesting insect.

The fiercer aspect of Kali danced in the Sister's eyes as she said, "Jason is a child when he drinks. Why do you young women encourage him in his weaknesses. I offered you my hospitality."

Lynn finally got angry. "It certainly wasn't my idea. I was going to shower because I couldn't sleep." She could tell she wasn't believed. She got up to go down the hall and pick up her things scattered near the doorway to the bath.

The Sister followed her and motioned her to come into her office. Once inside, again in the shadows with candle light, the Sister pulled at her sleeve and whispered harshly, "He is understandably angry at your...friendship with our Marta. Why are you so foolish, coming here like this? You step into the scorpion's path deliberately. One would almost think the Buffalo demon sent you to test him. He may fail the test if he sees you again."

A familiar experience. The woman was actually blaming her, Lynn, for Jason's intimidating behavior. Or maybe she knew and wanted to get rid of Lynn too? Had Jason 'failed the test' and gotten rid of Marta, carried her off somewhere and...? Lynn clutched the folded envelope in the pocket of her robe and said, rather too angrily, "I'm sorry for whatever trouble you feel I may have caused you and your followers. I'll write a letter to forward to Marta and then leave."

She hurried to her room to stuff her things into her bag. Then she sat down to write the note, knowing already that she wouldn't get an answer.

It began to rain as she got in her car. Was that Jason staring out a window at her? She started the engine and noticed something moving out of the corner of her eye—a red shadow moving quickly near the main building then toward her car.

She felt terror for a moment. The sword wielding arms of the goddess seemed to wave threateningly around a red figure. Kali? Then the mirage was gone. Some sort of cruel theatrical joke of Jason's, distorted by the raindrops on her windshield and the glare of her headlights? She didn't stop to investigate. She drove away quickly.

Although she kept reassuring herself that the Kalimayas were dedicated to helping people and wouldn't have harmed her, the image of Marta lying dead somewhere haunted her on the long, dark drive back. Like Sam, Marta had gotten in the way and.... She couldn't bear the thought. If only she had called Del sooner. If only she had looked for Marta sooner. When she left the first time. She would not believe that Marta was dead. She fought the tears. It was bad enough to have to fight to stay awake with the glare from the wet pavement and the passing cars. She felt very relieved when she saw the lights of Hartfield up ahead. She would find Marta before it was too late, even if it meant going to Nepal.

10

Del had called Lynn's office while Lynn was at the Kalimaya's north country retreat; her message on the answering machine said, "Thought you'd like to know. Somebody by the name of Marta Handley traveled straight through to Kathmandu on the twentieth of September. Seems like she got on the plane with two other people, one with a U.S. passport traveling under the name Margaret Jones and one with an Indian passport, a Rajid Singh according to the ticket agent. Nobody would swear that either of the women was the one in the photos you gave us of Marta, but nobody said it wasn't."

She returned Del's call, "She wouldn't have gone with them voluntarily."

"Hard to kidnap somebody and take them on public transportation," Del said dryly.

"There are other kinds of coercion."

Lynn filled Del in on her experience at the Kalimaya's rural retreat.

All Del said was, "Sure would have been good to get copies of those letters and receipts."

Annoyed, Lynn said, "I know, but there just wasn't a copy machine handy." Words from Marta's letter hung in the air above her left eye. *Fasting and meditation have not dispelled my fear of our involvement with these men....*

"What about the woman they call The Sister," Del persisted. "Too bad we don't know her real name so I could run a make on her."

Now Lynn remembered the Sister's look of worry and her voice saying, "...Can't see the flower because you are looking for a worm." Had the Sister been worried about bad publicity or was she fully aware of possible illegal sources for their funding? She told Del, "The woman was upset when I told her I had seen Marta. She wouldn't believe that Marta came to my apartment. Thought Marta was still in Nepal. It's hard to believe she is so ignorant about who was at the leadership meetings. She could have been lying I guess. Or maybe Marta had found out something she wasn't willing to discuss with the Sister."

"She must know something. Sounds like she might have sent Marta to Asia to resolve trouble there. Maybe even something that is behind Sam Jenson's death."

"And she found out what was going on there and came back to do something about it. She just never got a chance to talk to me...or you about it."

Then Del added quietly, "I hate to say it, hon, but maybe they sent her out of the country because she is still a murder suspect. Those letters are our best lead so far. If you could find Marta, we might be able to get some real information."

If she's still alive, Lynn thought desperately. "I'm convinced that Marta went to that meeting trying to stop the Kalimaya from involvement in illegal trade. If she wasn't kidnapped, all I can hope is that she found some place safe in Nepal. I've got to do something before she ends up like Sam."

"Then why didn't she go to see that woman, her guru, to warn her?"

"Marta told me she could handle it herself. Maybe she did and that's why she went back to Asia."

Del sighed loudly. "I'm afraid that's just wishful thinking, hon. Get some evidence, blow their cover. If she isn't playing their game you'll be doing her a favor. If she is...."

Lynn sighed. "I know. If Marta lied about her involvement, used me for cover, or even killed Sam.... I'll still have my story. Do you think it was really Marta who got on that plane?"

"There's one way to find out for sure."

Lynn was silent for a moment while the idea sank in. "You mean go to Nepal?"

"Well, the department's not going to send me, that's for sure. Your boss at the *Chronicle* might be behind your going, anything for an exclusive. You've got addresses there. Go, look around. I'll do what I can from here. Maybe you can expose a drug connection. Thomas got some stuff on that guy, Jason. Got something of a record. Ex-addict. No evidence that he isn't clean now, though. Could be one of Marta's rescue jobs. Or maybe he's running a drug line from Asia and using the Kalimayas as cover."

Lynn hung up the phone slowly. Del's information gave her a strand of hope. Marta was alive, might even have left the country again on her own. But if that was true, why had she come to Lynn looking for help, promising information, and then left for Nepal without a word? It didn't make sense. What happened between that last phone call from Marta and...? Who were the people on the plane with her? And had Marta really gone voluntarily or...?

Bill was watching her from the door of their office, probably tired of the total chaos in his half of the room—papers, magazines everywhere, stacked in piles on the floor. She imagined him hoping she'd go out so he could spread his mess onto her desk. He lifted a pile of folders off a chair and sat down. "What'll you do now?"

She wasn't sure herself what she wanted to do. If she was working on a story, she'd be able to search for Marta. But what if Marta really was mixed up in something? Did Lynn want to be the whistle blower? "Ask Gale if I can follow the story to Nepal, I guess," she reluctantly answered to herself as well as Bill.

Bill nodded, the corners of his mouth pulled down in thought. "She just might do it. I can see the headlines now—*Hartfield Reporter Breaks International Case*." He laughed. "Good luck kid."

• • •

She called Peter, gave him the update and got permission to use his background material in her proposal. He would take care of this end, keep her informed. Whatever came up they would give jointly to the media. He would work with Del and Rog and whomever necessary on this side.

Then he said, "I did some more research on Allen and Gruber at the bar across the street from their storefront. Gruber is illegally in the US. Got caught with a stolen religious painting on his way through customs. He runs their European operation. Some sort of expert on archeological treasures. I'll keep working on this angle. If you hit pay dirt I will be there in twenty-four hours with whatever support you need. You find anything out once you're over there, you can count on me to back you up. "

"Thanks Peter. I'll get back to you after I talk to Gale."

Then holding her breath, Lynn went into Gale's office.

"O.K., spill it. I can smell a story a mile away just like my daddy, rest his soul."

Lynn nervously tried to find the right words.

Gale tapped her pen impatiently, "I can see you got problems. We'll talk about it over lunch. You look like you've been living on cigarette butts or something."

At lunch Lynn watched while Gale read through her proposal. Along with Peter's background research, Lynn had included what she remembered of the letters she had seen in the Sister's office together with copies of the stuff she had dared to steal from the Sister's desk and waste basket. Gale stirred her pasta, absentmindedly dumping cheese on it. The woman had a mind like a hungry tiger; she could read and remember everything.

Gale patted Lynn on the shoulder, probably her version of her own father's back-slapping style, and said, "Two weeks. I'll take you off the routine for that long. If all you get is a travel piece about Americans in Asia and a bit about that Kalimaya retreat, so be it. Now go for it, keep me posted, and call in every two days."

11

With the help of the *Chronicle's* office manager, Lynn managed to get the shots she needed, an update on her passport and make her flight in two days. There was little time to worry about Marta.

She leaned back in the plush seats of the wide-bodied jet. Plenty of extra seats to stretch out on later if she should want to nap after supper. She loved traveling, had even done a few free lance travel pieces, but this was her first assignment tied in with an unsolved murder case. She studied some papers that Peter had given her on the current activities of the Society. There were hints—a member arrested with drugs—an office in California with a suspicious stone goddess.

They claimed it to be a replica of the original. But the original was missing from its temple in India. The experts hadn't been able to verify it as a copy yet. She put the pages in her bag but couldn't sleep. She began worrying about Marta. How much did she know? Had Jason been lying when he said that Marta deliberately took advantage of Lynn? She was pretty sure someone had killed Sam because he was going to talk. Didn't that mean Marta's life was in danger as well?

One stop in London to exchange passengers. Time enough for a cup of sweet tea with too much milk.

Back on the plane there were Indian families fashionably dressed in Western style among the business people and tourists. She was about to stretch out for a nap when she noticed an Indian man across the aisle watching her over his newspaper. He smiled and handed her an extra blanket, saying when she hesitated to take it, "Not to worry. I won't need it. No problem." She took it and tried to sleep. She was beginning to see trouble everywhere, even in a friendly gesture.

Something woke her—an extra bump of the plane? The lights were still dimmed. Had her handbag been on the empty seat next to her? She remembered it being securely under the seat in front of her. She looked across for the man who had spoken to her and given her the blanket. His seat was empty. She switched on the overhead light and looked in her bag. Nothing seemed to be missing, but she felt sure someone had searched the contents. Were some of Peter's xeroxes missing? She couldn't be sure.

She got up and walked around the cabin, but didn't see the man from across the aisle anywhere. The toilet cubicles were empty. Now she wasn't even sure she had seen him get on the plane. She smiled to herself. OK, maybe she had moved the bag herself and had forgotten about it. She was already making a B movie thriller out of everything on this trip.

• • •

During a stop in Kuwait, turbaned Sikh workers and women in gorgeous silk saris joined them. When Lynn got back on the plane, the Indian man was back in his seat, but now he had a turban carefully wound around his head like the other Sikhs. Her paranoid self got the better of her and she said to him, "Thank you for the loan of your blanket," as she held it out to him.

There was no recognition on his face. "I'm sorry, you have made some mistake. I have just entered the plane."

Lynn went to her seat flustered, feeling like an American tourist who can't tell foreigners apart. Annoyed, she went back to sleep, this time with her head on her bag.

By the time the plane landed in India, where she had to go through customs and change planes for Nepal, she was sure she had been traveling forever. Time was completely confused and her state of mind matched the hazy heat of the sky outside the concrete terminal. Was it morning? Now among the Indian families and English tourists that waited with her were enthusiastic English and French trekkers in sturdy leather hiking boots. Their practical clothing contrasted with the delicate open sandals, flowing silks, and fragile jewelry of the Indian women.

On the plane to Kathmandu—finally. The almond-eyed stewardess in Nepali dress served her curried pastries and tea as she watched the tiny dry-patch fields of the Indian plains give way quickly to foothills with scattered trees. What was that strange rim of clouds on the horizon? Suddenly she realized she was seeing a vast chain of mountains above the layer of clouds that hid the tops of the foothills below. Even though she knew they were the highest mountains in the world, she hadn't been prepared for their majesty. The Himalayas! Jagged ice spires, they stretched across the sky.

Finally, the conversation of the two men in the seats next to her pulled her awareness back into the plane. They were talking about the hydroelectric plant and dam that the World Bank was building in Nepal. She could imagine the power of the melted water cascading down from those immensely high glaciers. She could see, snaking between the trees, the paths of rivers that cut through the foothills below.

Soon they began to descend into the Kathmandu valley. Here the trees on the steep hillsides were replaced by the yellow, green and brown of rice terraces. Scattered here and there were two-story red brick houses. A real life Shangri-La, lush and beautiful. She saw no factories, no electric poles, no machine-filled roads on the steep slopes until they approached the city.

The hazy, hot reality on the ground contrasted sharply with the illusion of a mountain paradise. It was easy enough to get through the low dusty airport. She even felt welcomed by the young soldier who took her passport and entry fee and asked her if it was true that everyone in America was rich.

After going through customs, she made a reservation in the airport for an inexpensive, Western-style hotel. Then she was ushered out of the terminal by a young man clutching a pink piece of paper. She could only guess that the pink slip of paper had her destination written on it. A few rather beaten up cars waited on the unpaved road outside, surrounded by a crowd of boys. She watched helplessly as they passed the tiny piece of paper hand to hand.

At last an officious young Indian disappeared it into his pocket and directed her to an old blue Datsun. The boys who had taken charge of her baggage stuffed it into the trunk. Meanwhile, the Indian had opened the door for her and was talking in a staccato voice to the driver who sat silently smiling at her as if she had cake on her nose or something.

She shrugged and gave herself over to their charge, getting into the back seat. Immediately she was sorry as the whole crowd of boys began to push-start the car while her driver continued to look back at her and grin. Miraculously the car did start and they proceeded towards the city, at a clip that guaranteed the maximum effect of the potholes on her spine, down a narrow rutted road, bordered by rice fields .

The jostling competition between pedestrians, cows and motor vehicles struck Lynn as being the national sport. The pedestrians and cows ambled down the road unconcerned, while the cars, motorcycle tractors, buses and trucks honked continuously. They drove through the crowds, not quite knocking anyone over, just pushing a bit when necessary. Her driver seemed to have an uncanny ability to judge whether the living creatures he was about to ram would actually move out of the way or not. With considerable use of the questionable brakes, and without killing his engine, they managed to wend their way through the narrow streets to her hotel.

Merchants, among their piles of bottles and pots, peered out at her through low doorways. Women swept dirt from their stone doorsteps into the refuse-cluttered streets or washed clothes on the stone steps of small temples.

Everywhere there were temples with their resident stone deities covered with flower petals, globs of food, and red powder. Many people had red marks or flower petals and rice stuck to the center of their foreheads. She asked the driver what they meant. He grinned at her and told her in fair English that they were Tikas, "For good luck. Festival of Lights is over now. You just missed."

She got out of the car in the courtyard of the white stucco and tile hotel. The courtyard, unlike the streets, was actually paved, relatively clean and even had flowers blooming in pots along the rather high fence. The room she got could have passed inspection by the most scrupulous Dutch grandmother.

Lynn decided to stay awake until dark even though it was still the middle of the night back in the U.S, eleven hours difference. She had traveled almost half way around the world.

She dutifully clipped her money belt around her waist, carefully hung the two cameras she had brought securely across her shoulder and chest, got directions from the smiling young man at the hotel desk and started toward the center of town.

Now she was on the other team in the game of dodge-cars. She studied the technique of people in the street. Important to stay in the middle of the narrow streets because of the random offal along the side and the liquids that occasionally came from upper stories. It was clear that most people did not have the benefit of modern plumbing. Maybe she could make her fortune selling garbage cans to the Nepalese. She imagined herself the owner of a fleet of garbage trucks keeping the city pristine. But then many of the streets were too narrow for anything wider than a bicycle. Garbage bicycles, that was it. She would go to the World Bank. If there was money for dams...?

But behind the dust and the souvenir venders, the city was exquisite.In spite of the dust and noise, the smoke and carbon monoxide, the smells and the dirt—there was magic. Some of the wooden buildings with their delicately carved facades looked as if they were trying hard to return to the earth. Had the people been shorter in the old days or were the buildings sinking under the weight of age? Carefully carved goddesses held up the roofs of temples. On every street corner there was a small shrine with fresh flower petals and rice paste. Even in the middle of a narrow cobbled street a sacred stone had fresh offerings.

Lynn joined the happy sounds of a chanting crowd at a colorful Buddhist wedding with shaven headed priests magnificent in their saffron robes.

In a wide square with many temples and people selling tourist goods spread out on the stones, Lynn caught a flash of peacock blue silk. Marta? She was exhausted, imagining things, but she hurried after the woman in blue with a sense of desperation.

On the other side of the square, people were selling fruit and vegetables. The woman in the blue sari stooped to buy oranges. Lynn hurried over. The woman turned her head—not a Nepali, but she was also not Marta.

• • •

Back at her hotel after sleeping for at least twelve hours, Lynn ate a good breakfast and started out fresh. She picked up a guide book and asked directions at the desk to the address on Marta's letter, then took a taxi to Borabadur, a smaller and quieter city in the Kathmandu valley.

She took time for a few photos as she followed the directions, walking past wooden and brick buildings, past temples where stone gods and goddesses were blotched with bright red and orange offerings. Children ran about everywhere. A woman placed some rice paste on the stone face of the elephant-headed god, Ganesh. A moment later, a child snatched the paste and popped it into her mouth.

Lynn hurried on, down the narrow street of this sacred city of death toward the river where the thick smoke of incompletely burned funeral fires with their smell of charring flesh nearly choked her.

She passed well-dressed Hindu visitors from India, haggling with a flower merchant over the price of an offering. The flower seller turned toward Lynn smiling, the Western tourist. Lynn paid too much for a handful of fading flowers and went on past scores of people eager to sell her their trinkets.

Soon she stood in a cluster of small temples near a bridge. Nearby an old man sat sunning himself in a doorway, his head propped up with a curved stick braced against his knees. Had he come here to die and be burned in this sacred place? How strange to sit here every day watching the smoke rise from the funeral pyres so near.

Down river, monkeys played with drying laundry that was laid out on stepped stone walls. A crowd of bored residents gathered watching the monkeys play hide and seek under a shirt as a young girl ran to rescue her laundry.

Near Lynn, a small boy entertained himself by throwing bits of soft brick broken from the bridge at a monkey and its tiny baby. The bridge was pitted from such borrowings. How many small boys will play this game before the bridge falls, she thought.

She rested for a moment away from the cramped streets contemplating a collection of small temples lined up neatly among the trees on the other side of the bridge where cows tried valiantly to chew on the close-cropped and dusty grass.

Again she saw a flash of sea blue—the special blue of Marta's favorite sari. No doubt it belonged to one of the rich worshipers here to leave an offering at the Shiva temple with its massive gold bull god. Still, the sight made Lynn hurry across the bridge to the open grass where water buffalo and monkeys ruled. But it was only the long blue tail feathers of the tropical kingfisher.

She retraced her steps and asked some of the venders on the street to help her find the address she had found in the Sister's wastebasket. They pointed to a massive old Buddhist temple compound. Inside she found it to be a refuge for homeless people lined up for the daily meal.

Gale had suggested she hire a guide and translator, but she wanted to keep a low profile, look like a tourist. So far she had found people who were eager to practice their English. She put an offering in the box and showed a monk the address. The man looked concerned but shook his head.

She went back to the man who had directed her there and convinced him to come and translate for her. He talked to the old monk for a moment and then said. "She hasn't been here for a long time. She used to come with food and clothing for the women. When you find her ask her to come back. There are many who need her help."

Lynn smiled to herself. This certainly didn't look like a den of thieves and drug users. It was the sort of place that the Marta she knew would have worked.

Back at her hotel she made her first check-in phone calls to Peter and Del. To Del she exclaimed, "I've made my first contact with someone who knows Marta."

"Good work, girl," came the fuzzy voice over the great distance.

"Only trouble is he hasn't seen her for awhile, wants me to tell her to come back, so unfortunately he isn't much of a lead."

Peter advised her to go directly to the Kalimaya's retreat. "Don't bother with the peripheral stuff. Go straight into the lion's mouth. That's where you'll find the teeth. Just wander in, maybe they'll take pity on a poor lost tourist or something."

That night her excitement and nervousness made it impossible to sleep, so she wrote a travel piece, mostly to keep her head clear, keep her mind working. In the morning she mailed it with her roll of film to the *Chronicle*.

With the help of two backpacking trekkers, she found the right government building and stood in line for the necessary travel permit; then went to buy a ticket that would get her to the part of the country where the Kalimaya's had their retreat.

The Indian woman at the travel agency looked at her impassively for a long moment after she made her request for transport to the part of Nepal where she could find the Ashram.

Lynn pointed out the location of the Kalimaya's' retreat on the map. The woman responded with, "That is in the Terrai. Do you wish to visit the game park? There are several tours." The woman handed her a brochure with elephants and tigers on the cover.

Lynn smiled. "No. I just want to visit someone in the area. Is there a flight there?"

"We can arrange for a flight, but that point on the map is very far from an airport. Private planes...." she started to rummage through her pamphlets.

"Can't I just rent a car."

The smile disappeared. "We don't rent cars here, actually. It is very far and the mountain roads on the way there are steep...." She pulled out another pamphlet and smiled reassuringly. "Some of our tours have vans that can take you most anywhere. We have a tour that is just a week and takes in much of the area you have indicated. You would spend several days in the game park then—"

"Isn't there a van that can just take me where I want to go? Perhaps I could find a driver...?"

The woman shrugged. "A tour is less expensive. Actually, one needn't go to the expense of hiring a private car; one can purchase a tour on public transportation and arrange to be left in the village nearby. No problem."

Lynn packed a small backpack, left her luggage and valuables locked in the hotel safe, and left a message for Del with the hotel manager. She got up early the next morning to go down the dusty street to the market place to catch the bus.

It turned out that the tour consisted of being escorted by a small boy who found her standing confused among the crowds next to the collection of public buses in the market place, purchased her ticket and ushered her onto one of the buses. Finally securely in her place on the wooden seat, she watched the hot tropical landscape pass by the dusty window—towns of brick, wood and mud houses, terraced rice and green vegetable fields filled the valleys in an exquisite patchwork design beneath the haze of cooking fires.

As the bus barreled along, Lynn envied the total relaxation of the sleeping boy collapsed against her shoulder. Would he wake up in time to tell her the correct place to get off as he had promised?

Soon the road began to climb, winding tightly up steep slopes. One more curve in the road...and one more...there were so few trees to hold the earth to the mountain sides. A truck on the side of the road had its nose pointing safely toward a stone wall. She tried not to wonder how many vehicles made it to their destination on these steep narrow roads.

Her back began to ache. Surely there would be at least some sort of hotel somewhere along this road. What she wouldn't give for the worst of the freeway rest areas back home. She didn't dare eat any of the food thrust into her face through the window when the bus slowed at one of its interminable village stops. Hot, cramped, thirsty, miserable...why was she here, following a woman who hadn't even cared enough about her to leave a note?

Suddenly Lynn realized that part of the reason she was here in Nepal was that she wanted to tell Marta to her face how angry she was. Here she was, bouncing around on a hard wooden bench in a bus with no toilet, trying to find a woman who had not even the courtesy to say good-bye.

Then she remembered Marta's dark eyes, her sweetness and her generous spirit. She didn't want to be angry. She wanted Marta to be there at the retreat, safe and beautiful as ever with all her mysteries and contradictions.

After endless winding through more and more mountains, the bus finally came to a steamier and reassuringly flat countryside with wide stretches of fields.

The bus stopped at what seemed like just one more widening of the road with a few clay and stone huts, tea and pastry venders among the tailors at their sewing machines. She was assured by the boy who had miraculously awakened that she had reached her destination and was led to an ancient jeep where a young man seemed to be the only one who could read her incomprehensible piece of paper from the travel agent.

He motioned for her to climb in the back, trying to help her with her bag which she didn't quite release, feeling painfully foreign as she entrusted herself to him.

She had failed to notice when she got in the jeep that it had a flat tire. How long before the ancient wreck, presumably hired to take her to the retreat, could be nursed back to health? She watched as all the male inhabitants of the neighborhood contemplated the problem of repairing the truck tire. *How many Nepalese does it take to change a tire?* she thought crossly, giving up any attempt to be culturally sensitive. *Answer, Everyone within walking distance.*

She changed the film in her camera for the entertainment of the children gathering around her. That did not seem to distract them for long from their demands for pens and rupees. Her initial mistake had been to give away all her small change and pens. It had just whetted their appetite. A mother brought her baby over and pointed at Lynn. Lynn didn't understand the words she said, but it was clear from the frightened wide-eyed stare of the baby that he was seeing a creature from another world.

And it seemed as if it might take forever to get the jeep going. Besides, like every other vehicle here, the radiator leaked. Even if they left right away, with picking up passengers and water stops, going by jeep might take just as long as walking. Followed by her retinue of children, Lynn went to the jeep's driver and said, "How far to the retreat?"

He smiled and shook his head. "It is best you wait. No problem. You can buy a coffee-milk, just there." He nodded toward a stall down the street where people gathered around a few tables.

She tried again. "Which way will we go to get to the retreat?"

He pointed down the two lane road into the murky distance. She could see nothing but rice fields and wood smoke.

"If I walk, how long will it take me to get there?" she demanded, hot and hungry. She was not in a good mood.

He frowned and looked up into the sky as if the answer could be found there. Patiently, knowing she must struggle to find a way to ask the right question, Lynn said, "Would it be an hour's walk?" His frown deepened as he stared at his watch. His head moved back and forth slightly. That code wouldn't be in the dictionary. Maybe it meant that his watch didn't work and needed new batteries. Not a polite thing to ask about. "Would it take more than fifteen minutes?"

He bobbed his head, smiling, clearly relieved at a question he had an answer to. She assumed he had understood her and the answer was yes.

"Less than an hour?"

He looked down at the pavement as if seriously searching for the answer there. Finally he said, "That might be so."

Close enough—an hour she could manage, even in the hot sun. She smiled. "I will walk. Thank you."

She paid him his fee for the trip, but he still looked at her with a worried expression. "The Ashram is near the road isn't it?" she asked.

His smile broadened. "You will see the house of Kali near the road. You must ask the way."

His smile reassured her. She started down the road. At first, there were the dusty mud-packed stalls and houses of the village on either side of the hot pavement. She shared the edge of the road with heavily loaded bicycles, people with loads on their backs and school children in their blue cotton uniforms, bright white shirts and brown satchels.

Then there was nothing but silence and the stretching rice fields on either side, weeds and hot pavement, disturbed only occasionally by the dusty, rattling passage of trucks and buses. What was she doing here? Now that she was close, she wasn't sure she wanted to see Marta. Just another chance to get her feelings hurt. She felt stupid being on foot in this flat steamy insect ridden... She imagined herself dying of heat prostration, lying in one of the ditches, being chewed on by rats.

She shuddered and looked at her watch. Only fifteen minutes since she left the village. Not time to panic yet. What does a retreat look like? Would she know it when she saw it?

She passed a few isolated tiny farmhouses with mounds of rice-straw raised out of reach of the munching buffalo, carefully tended flowers and squash growing on the thatch roof. She spied an old woman sitting quietly near a well, and always the small children, smiling, surrounded her. She found a group of adults cutting rice in the field and asked them directions. They waved her on smiling. Had they understood her questions?

Then she could see a low hillside rising out of the flat fields ahead where there were actually trees growing. She entertained herself the last few feet wondering what kind of plants would be growing there. To be sure, it had to be something prickly that could survive the devastating mouths of the grazing animals that plagued all uncultivated space. Here and there were scraggly plants of the kind that people at home considered exotic house plants. She wondered how all those people would feel about their precious plants knowing they were weeds here.

At the foot of the hill near the road were two huge trees. As Lynn got closer, she could see that they were growing out of the remains of a small temple. These must be two of the sacred peepul or bo trees that she had read about, the sacred fig trees that were planted when a temple was built. The stones of the temple had been lifted from their foundations and were intertwined in the roots and trunks of the trees.

Tired and hot, she sat down on the stone step in the shade of one of the peepul trees where she could peer deep inside the temple. In the darkened interior she saw fresh offerings of flowers and red paint on a carved stone figure. She imagined the crude carving as the goddess of hot and weary travelers.

An old woman came slowly out the doorway of a hut beyond the temple making gestures at Lynn's feet. Lynn stepped away remembering that one was not supposed to enter with leather shoes on.

Assuming the woman would know no English, she said, "Kalimaya retreat," as clearly as she could. Unsmiling, the woman made one short jerk of her head toward a dirt track as if to say, go that way. Lynn went in the direction indicated. Soon she came to two stone lions guarding the gate of a new wooden fence. It was not locked. Perhaps it was only to keep the cows out. As if to confirm that thought, she saw large, thriving bushes of generous green with red flowers planted at intervals along the fence inside the gate. Geraniums!—what a good sign. Those bright red petals were almost synonymous with the Kalimaya Society. The thought of Marta further on excited her too. She went through the gate making sure to close it securely after her.

Someone had bothered to remove all the weeds along the road. There even seemed to be an attempt to plant grass— perhaps to establish the feel of an English country garden? Now there were banana plants and papaya trees and other plants she didn't recognize in the clearings along the road. They were small but carefully watered. Interspersed were figures of stone gods and goddesses. At what cost had they been collected?

Ahead she could see a cluster of thatch-covered wooden houses not that different from those she had seen from the bus. Unlike those in the villages with their packed dirt courtyards, however, they were laid out symmetrically, each in the middle of a carefully-tended square of grass surrounded by shrubs and flowers. Beyond them were larger thatch-covered buildings.

A tall man, long haired and bearded, wearing only a white cloth wrapped around his middle, Indian fashion was watering banana trees near some buildings. He did not look up until she was close enough to call to him. Then he contemplated her with what one could only describe as beatitude on his sunburned face. She asked for Marta and he slowly nodded his head as if she had said something wonderfully profound. Then he said something in what sounded like German and gestured back up the road from which she had come.

She smiled and went on, hoping she would find someone who spoke a language she could understand. She went into the first of the larger buildings. Inside the only light came through holes in the lattice of bamboo that made up the walls under the wide expanse of thatch roof. Once her eyes adjusted to the dimness, she could see that this was a dining room with the tables set up for a meal like a hotel, minus the bar. There were no people here, although she could hear a bustle of pots and pans and voices beyond a curtained doorway at the back.

She went back outside. Banana Man was gone. She went around the building to the back and found an outdoor kitchen. A Nepali woman was hunched over the clay stove. Others were chopping vegetables. A puppy came up to her, tail wagging, and she petted it. They watched her, smiling and she asked them if they knew where to find Marta. They only giggled. She squatted down and scratched the puppy's belly.

God, she was hot and tired. She tried mimicking someone very thirsty, drinking water, and was rewarded with a green coconut with a straw in it. She sat down on one of the numerous wicker chairs in the shade of a tree and sipped the cool sweet juice gratefully.

She shut her eyes for a moment, then heard a new voice from the front of the building. Lynn hurriedly tried to remember some German...French? Didn't all German's speak a little French? She approached them slowly, thinking, Voulez-vous....

Lynn realized the woman was speaking English and good solid Western U.S. English at that. "He said we couldn't get the bus before ten o'clock in the morning. We could get the van when it's fixed. What do you think, Charley? A couple days more here...take the river trip; or shall we bag it and...?"

Banana Man had a name, Charley. And now he was staring at Lynn. Was that a crinkle at the edge of his eye? He was enjoying his joke of not understanding English.

The woman speaking to him turned. An older woman dressed in jeans and short-sleeved plaid shirt, she had the delicate freckles and pink skin that said her white hair under her practical straw hat had once been red.

Lynn walked closer. "So he does speak English."

The woman turned to Charley who had gone back to watering his bananas. "Have you been teasing this nice young lady?" She held out her hand to Lynn and said, "Sue Jackson. This is my son Charley. He has my Wyoming sense of humor. From the looks of you, you just walked from Bombay."

Lynn shook hands with Sue. "I'm Lynn Evans. And not quite Bombay; I just walked from the village down the road. The vehicle I hired needed a tire fixed."

Sue guffawed. "And you wanted to get here before Tuesday. The local buses will pick you up if you wave like crazy, and they go all the time."

"I don't speak the language."

Sue shrugged. "You can always find a nice young man who wants to practice his English." She turned to the bearded giant behind her, scolding him as if he was still three. "Shouldn't tease like that, Charley. The poor kid's exhausted." She turned back to Lynn. "You a visitor like me or one of the inmates?"

Lynn felt confused, wary. What did she mean "inmate?" Lynn smiled wearily. "I'm just a visitor, looking for—or rather visiting a friend."

Charley volunteered, "Marta Handley is in retreat—up in the mountains, I hear."

His mother said sympathetically, "That sadhu man in the white suit will know more. You come over to my cabin and have a shower. I'll treat you to dinner later. After that, the guru swami or whatever they call him will be around with all his people."

"He has a name," Charley said, "Mr. Simpson will do. It's not that hard to remember."

"Back to your bananas, son." She grabbed Lynn's pack, slung it across her shoulder and started down the path.

Lynn hurried after her, finally feeling she was being taken care of and relishing it. They went into one of the huts. Lynn could see that the hut contained enough comfort—twin beds with sheets and a light blanket, a couple of shelves, two chairs and a small wooden table.

Sue placed Lynn's pack on the linoleum covered dirt floor and handed her a clean towel. "The showers are outside, just down the path next to the toilet. The water is as warm as the sun made it today but around here, wet is wonderful, warm or not. After you finish, you are supposed to pump the water back up. You'll see the pump. Come and get me and I'll show you how to do it."

As Lynn got her clean clothes out of her pack, Sue continued. "Back in the old days, we used to take cold baths in the horse trough. That was the only thing big enough to get into. No such thing as a shower in those days. 'Course, you could squat under the pump. Soap yourself up first, then get somebody to pump while you screamed with the cold and rinsed it off. Now we got a house with four baths, enough hot water to soak a horse. Takes all the fun out of it." She grinned heartily.

After a refreshing shower, Lynn sat with Sue on her little front step. Sue had hot lemon tea with lots of sugar waiting. Lynn took a deep breath and asked, "What did you mean when you called the people here inmates?"

"Well, you know, belly button watchers, people who spend

their time sitting around thinking about things rather than doing them. I'm a do-er myself. Nothing pleases me more than watching a room full of folks chompin' on fried chicken I cooked myself. Looks like you haven't had any fried chicken for awhile. You one of those veggies? My daughter Emily is one of those. I guess she saw me chop one too many roosters. Always hated pulling feathers, too. Now Charley, he's not a belly button watcher. Not any more. He did spend some time hangin' around the gurus. In India, you know. Traveled around on foot and all. He was somewhere on one of those rivers that run out of the mountains into the Ganges, the sacred river, you know, when I sent him the telegram. He's managing the family ranch now. A great relief for me now that my arthritis is acting up. Can't take more an half a day on horseback nowadays."

"Telegram?"

"Yeah, it said, 'Come home. We got oil.'"

Lynn heard a guffaw like Sue's only one octave lower. Charley came around the corner of the hut. "I thought she meant that the truck was leaking oil, or that the sunflower crop finally made it. "

Sue put her hand on his arm affectionately. "Charley runs the whole shebang now. We got three wells in Wyoming along with cattle and grain fields in Colorado."

Charley settled himself and accepted the cold drink his mother offered. He had on a clean, white, short-sleeved shirt and slacks that transformed him into an American businessman on vacation. The only thing that led one to suspect his spiritual leanings was the neatly trimmed beard with streaks of gray in it and the silver pendant of the four armed goddess of good fortune, Laksmi, hanging from a cord on his neck.

"What was the language you used on me?" Lynn asked.

His smile was more friendly now. "Hindi. I wanted to discourage you. Hoped you would go away. Tourists don't believe this isn't a hotel. If they hear a Western language, they think they can get a room for the night—especially since the nearest hotel is at least twenty kilometers away. By the way, it will get very dark here. You had better go soon if you want to make it back to the village before dark. There is usually a bus that goes by before dusk."

Lynn smiled. "I'll take that chance. I have to find Marta. I'll wait."

Sue frowned at Charley. "Son, where's your sense of hospitality gone? I thought I taught you better." She said to Lynn. "On the ranch, I always cooked enough so that we could feed anybody that came by. Out there we have a real tradition of hospitality. You always knew no matter how far out from home you were, there was a roof and a meal. "

Charley sighed quietly. "You know how they feel here about disruption by outsiders. Miss Evans will understand. This is a retreat. I will give her message to someone and Marta can contact her later. There are phones, you know, even out here."

"I'm an outsider too. I like having another outsider to chat with."

"You're my mother, not an outsider. You're here because I invited you."

Lynn was rooting for Sue. She said, rather pathetically, "I'm really concerned about Marta. I want to see that she is all right."

Sue patted her hand. "It's OK, hon. You can stay with me. There's an extra bed in my room and I'll treat you to dinner."

Sue scowled at Charley, but he persisted. "No one will tell you where she is. I'll speak to someone after meditation. Maybe a message can be taken to Marta for you."

Lynn asked, "Do you know Marta?"

Charley took a sip of his drink as if wanting time to decide what he should tell her. Finally he said, "I've seen her, though not recently. She's one of the inner circle that keep pretty much to themselves here."

"Why shouldn't they tell me where she is, if she isn't here? What are they hiding?"

"I told you, she's in retreat. They take the privacy that requires very seriously. They're protecting her. She will get in touch with you if she wants to see you."

That hit too close to home. What if Marta was just refusing to see her? Or hiding out because she had killed Sam? But then the fear in Marta's voice in that last phone conversation came back, the certainty in that voice that Marta would have something to report that would be important to Del. She could be a prisoner here if she was still alive, and all protest about how she was in retreat was just a cover-up. Was Charley just ignorant or was he in on it?

"If she doesn't want to see me, I intend to hear it from Marta." Damn, Lynn couldn't keep the tears out of her voice.

Charley got up. "I'll do what I can. You two have a nice chat before dinner. You'll have to be my cousin."

"I grew up in South Dakota if that's any help."

Charley smiled politely and left. Sue said, "Evans, I know some people by that name. Ranchers in Montana, any relation of yours? I got cousins in South Dakota name of Snow."

The light-hearted conversation that followed soothed Lynn's weary edges. Sue made her feel down-home and comfortable so that she almost forgot how far she had come. A few minutes later, the dinner bell rang.

"Now remember, they don't much like talking during dinner," Sue said. "What they got against talking beats me. It's an addiction with me after too many hours not talking, the men all out in the prairie, nothing but babies and horses for company. They come home and can't wait to fill their bellies."

"With your fried chicken," Lynn added.

"That was a satisfaction. Food here's not bad, nice and spicy, but for spice I prefer molé sauce or hot salsa any day. I'm here cause I was curious about the place. It's nice to have you here. Another nonbeliever. Somebody to talk to. Charley is a good boy, but he's just like his father, short on words."

The meal was a stew with incredibly tough meat. Lynn asked Sue if it was rhino meat.

Sue snorted and whispered. "Wouldn't surprise me a bit."

Local people were slipping in and out on silent feet bringing more food and taking away plates. There were twenty plus people in the dinning room. Most of them sunburnt Westerners. She heard German and Italian as well as English. Lynn noticed the massive bone structure of the Westerners compared with the graceful Nepali. She suddenly felt like an ugly giant even though she always thought of herself as slight, if not underweight.

After dinner there was talk at her table of the white rhino in the region. A youngish Nepali man in a camouflage suit was sitting across from Lynn. She wondered if the suit reflected a fashion or profession. He said, "They are coming into the fields at night and eating the tender seedlings. Even the ditches and fences don't keep them out anymore. "

Someone asked why the government wasn't taking care of the problem.

"They are protected because their habitat has shrunk so drastically. Being vegetarians, they are only dangerous when provoked. But in their presence, one must always be ready to climb the nearest tree. They are unpredictable and frequently charge, but having short memories, they soon wander away." He looked directly at Lynn. "It is always better not to go into the forests alone."

A dark heavyset bearded man in a white suit who had come up to their table said, smiling, "Let us hope the goddess Shakti will protect us from such demons."

He held out his hand to Lynn. "How do you do Miss Evans; I am Donald Simpson." She shook his hand as he said, "This evening there will be a lecture on the Asta Matrikas, the divine mothers, if you care to attend. It will explain some of our philosophy."

She smiled. "Thank you. Are you the one who will contact Marta for me? I am very anxious to see her. Perhaps you could direct me to where I can find her."

"Charles has explained your problem to me. Unfortunately Marta, as you call her, has asked not to be disturbed. That is a request we are bound to honor. I am sorry. But, not to worry, you are Mr. Jackson's guest for this evening and are welcome. There will be a bus in the morning that can take you back to Kathmandu. I'm sure Marta will contact you when she is ready. Just leave an address with me in the morning." He disappeared rather abruptly into the gathering darkness leaving Lynn angry and frustrated.

They retreated to Sue's porch with cups of tea. Sue watched her quietly for a moment and then said, "There's a rafting trip in the morning. Want to go? It's a two day trip ending on the river near here. Maybe there would be something from your friend by then."

Lynn thanked her. The extra time might make it possible to look around, and maybe they would get tired of seeing her and tell her how to find Marta. Although the idea of voluntarily putting herself in the middle of raging rapids was not one she relished.

Sue said, smiling, "I'll rope Charley into coming along."

Charley appeared out of the dark and said to his mother, "You do have a way of trying to arrange my life for me."

Lynn said, rather relieved that she might avoid the rapids, "I don't want to impose on your vacation any more than I have. You've been kind enough already."

Sue piped in, "Don't worry. It's not a favor. I can use the company. It gets a little tiresome being around all these 'Getting my head together people,' restful or not."

Charley smiled. "Actually, I've got business with the Baba. I'll go rafting with you after all." He turned to Lynn. "He's a priest that lives on the river. It's the easiest way to get there."

Sue asked, "What business?"

"Whatever you might think about this retreat, it is a responsibility of mine; I am a trustee. The Baba is an important local spiritual leader. I think our guests would be interested in having him visit here. I said I would speak to him about it."

Sue sighed and said to Lynn, "Anyway, it's settled. You're going with us."

So, tomorrow she would be, god forbid, rafting, an adventure she dreaded even in the name of finding Marta. But if Sue could go rafting at sixty, she could, too.

Two men came out of the dark and motioned to Charley.

She hadn't seen them at dinner. Where had they come from? She stayed in the shadows of the porch. One of them looked familiar.... Was it the Indian that had been watching her and offered her a blanket on the plane?

No, it was the man in the gray suit that had come to her apartment looking for Marta. Hijras, wasn't that what he had called himself? Trade the shirt and shorts for a suit, get rid of the beard....

She didn't recognize the other one—Should she tell Charley? But he might be in with them. At this point, she didn't know who she could trust. Charley might be their connection here in Nepal.

The two disappeared quickly down the path into the deep

132

black of the tropical night. Charley said, "Excuse me, I have a meeting. I'll see you at breakfast."

Sue was annoyed. "You could at least introduce me to your rude friends."

There was a brief bitter smile at the corner of his mouth. "You can be glad you don't know them."

Sue's voice grew angry. "If they are such bad sorts, what the hell are they doing here and why are you bothering to talk to them?"

"That's the sort of thing I'm planning to find out." Charley also disappeared into the dark.

Sue whispered under her breath, "I thought he was through with all that."

"All what?"

Sue was silent for a long moment, her face turned away. Then she said, "This place is cursed. I knew we shouldn't come here, that he shouldn't come back." She turned to Lynn, her face showing her tiredness in the yellow light of the lamp. "I don't know what he was doing those years here, but he made a living even then, a good living. I don't want to know. The faster we get back home the better I'll like it." She smiled and patted Lynn's shoulder. "We'll have a good time on those rapids tomorrow. Nothing like white water to cheer you up."

Lynn liked Charley. She didn't like the idea that he might be part of the problem. She had to find out for herself what those three were up to. "Have you seen those men before?"

Sue shook her head. "I might not remember all of Charley's old friends even if I did meet them once. Now, I don't know about you, but I'm for a good night's sleep."

"I'm going to take a little walk around to help me sleep. See you in the morning."

Lynn felt like a cat burglar. She had slipped on dark trousers and shirt before dinner. Maybe she should blacken her face in good spy fashion. But then if she were caught, there was no pretending she was just out walking. She went in the direction that she had seen Charley go.

In front of each cabin a freshly lit kerosene lamp waited for the occupants. At one end of a row of cabins the lamp was missing and she saw a glow coming from the open space below the roof. When she got closer she could see silhouettes in the lamplight, two figures sitting on the beds, two standing. She positioned herself next to a tree across from the small window. Four people in the room—the two who had come after Charley and someone else she hadn't seen. She could see only Charley clearly as he stood nervously by the door, talking. Lynn couldn't hear what he was saying. She moved closer, crouching under the window behind some shrubbery.

Charley's voice sounded resigned, angry and a bit shaky. "I'll say it just one more time. Get out now. Sign yourselves out of here quietly. Disappear. I know I made some mistakes in the past and you were one of them. That was a long time ago. I'm not the starving, empty headed kid you picked up on the streets of Bombay anymore. Get out now and I'll try to forget I ever knew you."

A southern voice answered, "Fat chance, Chuck old buddy. Look, get used to it. We're here to stay—genuine, certified recruits to your new-style Kali religion. I didn't sacrifice my precious time to get thrown out by a guy who can't figure where his interests lie. What's the matter old buddy? Gettin' soft in your old age? Or did the old gal, your ma, deprogram you? Is that why you gave up your Indian Guru fellow and went home? I wouldn't put it past the old bat. She couldn't wait to get you back into her clutches." He laughed.

Now a European spoke. Lynn couldn't recognize his accent. "It is naive of you to think that you can make any difference by trying to threaten us, Charles. You are not the only one who can help us; your precious cult is riddled with people willing to cooperate. Go ahead and hide your head in the sand."

Charley responded, defensively, "I don't believe you. I know our people in Kalimaya. You're wasting your time telling me such lies."

A third voice. She was sure she had heard it before. This time the accent was Indian. "We are wasting our time, actually. Whatever you now believe, what my friend here tells you is accurate. We have convinced enough followers that the Goddess will not mind a little profit in trade goods to be spent in her cause. Mr. Jackson will be given time to ponder our proposition. We will leave now. Mr. Jackson knows he has no choice but to be silent on this issue. Even if he does decide not to cooperate, we know enough about his past to assure his lack of interference in our business here. We will speak to him again before he leaves the country."

Charley was silent. What was this mysterious and profitable business? What had he done that made them so sure that he would cooperate?

There was a rustle as they got up to leave. Lynn stepped back from the building in such a hurry that she tripped, twigs breaking as she fell into the path. She scrambled up. She could see as she crouched in the bushes the three of them looking toward the window. They had heard her. She moved quickly away from the building her heart beating too fast. She decided that, if they came after her, she would say she had gotten lost on her way back from the john.

Fortunately the door was on the other side of the building. She stood in the shadows of another cabin to watch them leave. The Indian turned and held the lantern in her direction. The light did not quite reach her, though she couldn't be sure they hadn't seen her. Damn, what a bumbling fool she was. She hurried to Sue's hut not looking back.

Lynn was sitting out on the porch trying to get calm enough to sleep, when Charley came up out of the dark. He sat down next to her. "What did you hear?"

"What do you mean?"

"Let's not waste our time. I know you are a reporter and that you were snooping outside my door. A fact that could be unfortunate for you."

"Are you threatening me?"

"I'm not the threat. Even if you didn't hear anything, they'll assume you did."

"How did you find out who I am?"

"Donald Simpson knows. Somebody from back home must have warned him or maybe your friend told him."

" Marta doesn't know I'm here looking for her."

"Come on; tell the truth. You're here to dig up dirt on our organization."

"Not fair. I *am* worried about Marta, although of course it's true I got my paper to pay for my trip on the basis of a possible story. From what I heard it looks like there is one."

Charley sat in silence for a moment.

Lynn said, "Enough on you to keep you quiet? What were you doing back in your days of sitting at the feet of the guru?"

"Mostly selling uncut stones, a little jewelry and a little dope to pay for my chapatis."

Then Charley turned his head away. Lynn thought she saw him blush. "There was a time when what they know about me, my personal relationships...back when I was young and a bit crazy. Then I would have worried about keeping quiet. But now everybody that matters knows about me...and my sexual preference." He shrugged. "But let them think they can coerce me; maybe I can find out enough to nail them. Maybe I can do something once I am home, if I string them along for a while. It's difficult here. I'm not a citizen of Nepal."

"Sounds dangerous."

"And what you are doing isn't?"

"I'm just looking for Marta. "

"Lets hope they believe that."

"What are they actually trying to get you to do?"

"Not just smuggle a few pieces of art for them. I don't know exactly all that they plan, but I can imagine. They aren't in for the pennies. I'm a member of the governing board of the Society. Those guys lost the last show-down thanks to Marta and her efforts with the leadership. They don't want that to happen again."

"How bad is the Society's involvement now? Is the Sister...?"

"God damn you reporters! Just because a couple of crooks try to use us for cover."

"I'm sorry. If I can be of any help—"

"Those creeps are not part of our organization. They are trying to exploit us."

"And you can't do anything about it. Maybe you need my help. Maybe a newspaper article exposing them would help."

"Look, this place isn't safe right now. We'll get you on the bus tomorrow. I promise I'll let you know if there is a story."

"I've got to find Marta. I've got to warn her, get her out of this medieval place."

Charley looked at her for a long moment. "If I help you find her, will you leave?"

Lynn held her breath. "You know where she is?"

"I know someone who might."

Lynn let her breath out slowly. Charley leaned in closer. "We'll ask the Baba. He might tell you where she is." He smiled. "Who knows. It's even possible she's there with him."

"Why didn't you tell me before?"

Charley frowned. "I don't know your Marta very well, but I respect her work and her right to a meditative retreat. At this point, as far as I'm concerned, helping you is the lesser of two evils. Those guys suspect you. It's better to get you out of here before they do something stupid."

Lynn shuddered. So there was no way she was going to get out of this rafting thing. But maybe she would really find Marta. She felt the tears and turned away. What if Marta was angry and hostile at her intrusion? What if...?

12

L ynn didn't sleep well, dreaming of the fierce face of many-armed Kali with her necklace of skulls, holding a cup of blood. She was almost glad when Sue woke her up at dawn.

After an early breakfast of hot tea and soggy toast, the three of them joined a group of rafters collecting at the bus stop—pleasant enough young people in shorts, very sunburned, European, and embarrassingly healthy.

Sue said, "We have to go upstream to get to the real good rapids. The river is slow as a cow's cud down here."

As they pushed their way onto the bus. Sue proclaimed, "Always room for one more. Three people to a seat, or two Westerners with a small child between them."

Soon they were out of the flat lands, going up and up into the hills. After a while the bus began to follow the winding curves of a deep ravine. Lynn looked down into the mad dash of the water at the bottom with some trepidation. Watching Sue contemplate the rushing white water below with placid confidence made her feel much better. She tried to listen calmly to the exchange of rafting feats between the muscular young athletes shouting across the aisles. But she was grateful when the driver turned on his crackling PA system and she could concentrate on the loud Indian music filtered through a layer of scratch and static. She studied the lighted Krishna over the driver's head that blinked and dimmed with the short in its wiring.

When they finally reached their embarkation point, Lynn climbed down the bank and put on the worn life vest, picking up a paddle like the others and climbed into the raft as if this were an ordinary daily event.

When they were moving swiftly through what looked like healthy surf, one of her legs hanging over the side of the huge rubber raft and her paddle in hand, she realized what she was in for. She tried to concentrate on the calm voice that echoed somewhere in the hollow caverns of her mind: *Its only water and you can swim. Hundreds of people have done this before.*

When that didn't help, she concentrated on listening to the guides in the back of the raft shouting directions. She desperately tried to follow their example and dip her paddle at the right moment. The guides, two boys from the Sherpa tribe who looked as if they had graduated from the local version of Muscle Beach, seemed to know what they were doing. If they could lead treks into the Himalayas....

Then the rapids abruptly disappeared and they were on water that didn't even show white caps. She was just about to relax a little when the young Englishman sitting in front of her turned and handed her his underwater camera. "Mind getting a shot o' me and me mate with the whitewater? It's all automatic, self-winding," he reassured her. What was there to do but grin and nod and take the camera? He pointed out the right button as the next drop in the river loomed ahead. She put down her paddle, obediently kneeled in the center of the raft, placed her finger on the button, aimed the camera and closed her eyes.

It was a bumpy ride; she almost lost the camera overboard. But concentrating on taking pictures helped her to put the whole thing into perspective. She dutifully snapped the camera's owner madly paddling and even after giving the camera back she found herself looking forward to the next set of rapids.

And when they were in the fierce water, she paddled madly with the rest, exhilarated by the rush of white foamy waves that dipped and tossed them about like a cork. In the end she was almost disappointed when the steepest of the rapids were past and they had stayed afloat and right side up.

Charley had arranged with the guides that they stop early, so that he could take Lynn in a canoe to see the Baba. They left the main party setting up camp on a grassy cow field next to the river near a small village.

It was late afternoon after they passed the wide rocky spit where the Kali and the Gondaki rivers met. After a few minutes on the wider, quieter river they landed on a rocky beach. Was this to be the end of Lynn's search? All along the way she had imagined Marta as the wispy figure off in the distance, in the rice fields along the top of the cliff that lined the river here, or waving from the long curve of the suspension bridge that spanned the water a hundred feet above its swift current. Always the tiny figure was someone else.

From the river's edge Lynn looked up the steep narrow path to see an older, nearly naked man sitting under some trees as if expecting them. He was thicker than most Indians or Nepalese but he had a rather skimpy, long gray beard and hair knotted on top of his head like other priests she had seen on the streets in Kathmandu.

By the time she and Charley got up the path, breathless, others had joined the Baba to greet them. A very pretty, very young man with a large gold earring and chain around his neck over a shirt of leopard skin exchanged rather intimate smiles with Charley.

The Baba's other companion was a thin, smiling, dusty and sun baked sadhu with matted long hair and pilgrim's robes and beads. He was absorbed in the ritual of filling his clay pipe. Charley explained that the pipe was called a chillum, and that the smoking of hemp was the sacred privilege of the priests. The old man nodded and smiled at Lynn as she stood getting her breath back.

From here, the view of the river and the cliffs of damp jungle reaching steeply up from it on the other side was breathtaking. But their climb had not ended. The old man led them further up the path. When Lynn turned to ask Charley where they were going, she saw him disappear behind some trees with Leopard Boy.

After admiring the view and complimenting the Baba on his fruit trees, Lynn tried to question him about Marta. Though he spoke some rudimentary English, he didn't seem to understand what she was saying; he nodded agreeably to all her questions and waved his hand toward a long building nearby, "Visitors stay there." She walked over and looked inside imagining Marta there, but there was no evidence that anyone had lived there for some time.

Maybe he thought she had come to sit at his feet and learn his wisdom. Where was Charley when she needed him to translate for her? She tried to relax. There certainly had been times in her life when a week sitting in a warm sunny place eating bananas off the trees would have made her happy.

The old man motioned her to follow him again. Under the trees was an open temple with six small altars around the edges containing various carved stone Gods and Goddesses. Two young men were cooking a big pot of rice over an open fire in the middle. The Baba gave them orders imperiously, clearly the king in this small hillside paradise. They spread mats on the stone pavement, and she seated herself across from the Baba, again trying to question him about Marta. He silently repacked his pipe. The sadhu, still smiling, sat down near them rocking gently and smoking.

Lynn was suddenly conscious of the sound from the trees around her, the distinctive but strange bird songs, the rustling insects. A slight breeze moved the intensely green leaves. Dogs barked in the distance. The gold of late sunlight brightened the stone of the temple; she watched a spot of sunlight move across the face of a stone god.

"Shiva. She is Shiva." The words hung in the air between them. Was this Baba's English just bad or did he mean that this stone Shiva was in a female aspect?

She said, "It looks like figures of Buddha I have seen."

He shrugged and nodded. "All the same."

Lynn felt like Alice talking to the Caterpillar. And when was she going to wake up? As she watched him try again to light his pipe with a burning twig from the cooking fire, she tried to think of a way to ask her question so that he would understand. After what seemed like an eternity of silence, he smiled at his success in finally lighting his pipe. He held it out to her. Just then Charley came back looking somewhat pale. Leopard Boy was no longer with him.

Rather peevishly she said, "He doesn't seem to know who Marta is."

Charley accepted the pipe from the old man and then spoke with him in Hindi for a few minutes. Charley turned to Lynn. "He doesn't know her by that name. She is called Tika now. It's a word for good luck symbol. According to him she hasn't been here in a while."

Charley stared at Lynn. "You should know that he says that she has left the fold so to speak. She's no longer a member of the inner circle at the retreat. She has either left or been thrown out for some reason."

"You mean the story about her being in meditative retreat really was a lie?"

"That certainly is a possibility."

Did that mean Marta really was in trouble? She wondered if Charley was thinking the same thing.

"He says he can get you a guide to take you to the village where she is staying. It will cost you. And I can't guarantee that it isn't a scheme to make a little money."

"He is dishonest? "

"Honesty isn't the point. She probably has been there or will be there sometime. No doubt the people in the village can get a message to her."

She tried not to show her disappointment that Marta wasn't here. "Then I have to go there. I don't have any other leads."

He spoke to the Baba again. Then to Lynn he said, "You'll have to come back with money and stuff for the trail. He says it will take a couple of days trekking to get there. You can get back here by road in a day or so from the retreat. I'll help you get the stuff together. Who knows, maybe we can talk Mom into going along."

"You'll come with me?" She couldn't keep the gratitude out of her voice.

He smiled. "Can't let a greenhorn like you go into them thar hills alone."

Leopard Boy appeared at the bottom of the cliff and climbed into the canoe silently. Lynn looked over at Charley for an explanation, but he would not look in her direction.

Back at the camp, Sue asked outright why the boy was there. Charley smiled at her. Did Lynn detect some bitterness in that smile? He said, "Sorry Mom. It's just some of my far-out Tantric rituals. The young man is a fellow worshiper of Purusha. But I promise; he won't come home to Wyoming with us."

Lynn asked, "He doesn't happen to be another employee of

Asia Imports by any chance?"

Charley flushed. "I sincerely hope not. He may be a little crazy by local standards, but...he is a friend."

The next day the trip on the river was calmer. She had time to enjoy looking for birds and monkeys in the jungle-covered cliffs.

The only ominous thing was that Leopard Boy was in the boat and Charley was remarkably silent. The young man worried her, although he sat quietly in the back with the guides, chatting, laughing like any other adolescent with his buddies. Why did he scare her? Was it the obvious value of his jewelry? Was it so unreasonable to think that a teenager like that would be in school someplace if he had parents wealthy enough to afford such gifts? Or was the jewelry a way of flaunting that he was earning money in some questionable way?

And what was his relationship with Charley beyond the obvious? Was that what Charley meant when he talked about the crooks using his personal relationships against him? She would have to ask Charley more about him once they were beyond the roar of the river.

13

When they arrived at the compound, it was meditation time and there was no one around. Lynn and Sue retired to the cabin for a shower and a nap.

Sue seemed unusually subdued. Finally she admitted that she was leaving the next morning to go back to Wyoming. "And a good thing too. I've had enough of this infernal country. Nothing but dust and heat and hungry children, sick babies and dried-out cows. Charley can go trekking with you." Sue put her arm around Lynn. "I'm glad you'll have his company. Just do me the favor of seeing that he gets on the bus with you when you leave this place. I'd hate to have to come all the way back here to get him."

Lynn smiled at her. "I imagine Charley can take care of himself."

"I'm not so sure of that in this cursed country. It has an unnatural glow about it. Like something left out of the icebox too long."

"Is it the kid in the leopard skin you are worried about?"

Sue sighed and shook her head. "I've got used to the idea that he prefers male company and isn't likely to produce any grand-kids for me. His sister will pop 'em out for them both. I even like some of Charley's friends at home. That kid, though, I just don't trust him. He has the too innocent, pretty look of a critter that might jump out and bite you when you least expect it."

In the late afternoon Lynn was sitting out on the porch while Sue packed. She saw something out of the corner of her eye com-ing down the path in the dusky light, a streak of tropical blue. Not the right shape for a bird this time. Someone was coming toward her wrapped in the exact blue-green of Marta's favorite sari. Had Marta received her message and come to see her? Lynn stood up and hurried toward the blue apparition.

As she drew closer, she recognized Leopard Boy with a blue-green silk cloth twisted around his waist. She would have sworn it was Marta's with its distinctive hand-painted peacock design. She tried to control her disappointment as he stopped in front of her.

Then he motioned languidly for her to follow him. She couldn't keep the anxiety out of her voice. "Did Marta give that to you?"

He said nothing, but his eyes challenged her.

Should she risk it? Charley had called him a friend.

"Is she here?" She didn't even know if he spoke any English. He started to walk back down the path. She called out, "Wait." Was there time to get Charley?

The boy didn't even slow down. He was disappearing. She had to go after him; she might not get such a chance again. Lynn grabbed her flashlight and day-pack calling to Sue, "I think Marta is here and wants to see me." Then she hurried down a narrow dirt trail into the dusk.

Once outside the retreat's compound she was surrounded by women returning to their village with huge bundles of twigs precariously balanced on their back and suspended by bands around their foreheads. Little girls ran after her calling out their few English words and looking disappointed when, in her hurry, she ignored them. The blue-draped figure, far down the road that passed the retreat, was headed into a patch of jungle. She ran.

When Lynn got close enough to Leopard Boy to touch his arm, his brown eyes, highlighted by the golden glint of the setting sun, looked into hers. He nodded toward the trees. Then he disappeared into the darkening forest away from the road and its comforting presence of women.

Did she dare follow? She could go just a little way, she reasoned. If Marta wasn't there, she would go back and find Charley. She hurried after him.

She'd lost sight of him and was about to turn back when she was surrounded.

She screamed and tried to run as they went for her. The animal sound of her own voice echoed in her head. Had the women noticed her leaving the road? Would they report her disappearance? Why hadn't she stopped to find Charley? A gag went into her mouth as she struggled.

The vision of Sam's body slumped on the stairs in that decrepit hotel flashed before her. What had the poor guy known to be such a threat? What the hell did she know? Precious little to deserve this. The last thing she saw in the dim light, was a decorated cowboy boot with a pointed toe.

She was brought back to consciousness choking with rice dust and being knocked about with her hands and feet tied. They had stuffed her into an ox cart under rice straw.

She could hear noises, animals...trucks...shouts...the high-pitched squeal of wooden cart wheels under her during a bumpy ride. No one would be able to hear her squeaks and sneezes; there were too many road noises. She heard the whine of a rice-polishing mill, the noise of sewing machines in a village and always the voices, the crackling music. There was no way to keep track of time or where she was being taken. Through the straw and slats of the cart she saw the flickering light of court-yard fires, a glimpse of a small whitewashed shrine, children's faces in the distance. The cart tipped precariously as it took a sharp turn, and came to an abrupt stop.

Her captors dumped her into a small stone room, still gagged and bound, and left her in the dark. Was this a temple, shut and locked from outside? It smelled of urine and dust and was crammed with wooden crates. She tried to work the ropes off, or fray them by rubbing against edges of the carved stone window frame. All she managed was to loosen her hands enough so that she could relieve her bladder without getting too wet.

She tried not to panic. She could only hope that Sue would miss her and alert the authorities. Peter and Del knew she had left Kathmandu, but she wasn't due for a phone check-in for a couple of days. They knew there was no phone at the retreat. They had agreed that if she didn't check in, Peter would come looking for her. She had left stuff at the retreat and her valuables and notebooks were at the hotel in Kathmandu, so they would know she hadn't come back. On the other hand, she wouldn't be the first American to have abandoned a pack. After all she had her daypack containing some money and her passport with her.

By the time Peter found her trail it would probably be too late anyway. Charley, what about Charley? Would he give a damn? Maybe he was in on it. Maybe the whole Kalimaya Society was involved in some illegal shit, saw her as a threat, and had hired these thugs to get rid of her. Did that mean that Marta was already dead and they were trying to cover up?

There was always Sue. She would be worried—might do something. But Lynn had her daypack with her. Sue might think Lynn had just decided to give up and go home.

She imagined police questioning the women with the bundles. The little girls had also seen her. Would they pick up the trail in the woods? How thorough would Nepalese police be?

Eventually she dozed off, only to be awakened abruptly when her captors came back later—with food and beer. There were signs of dawn outside the barred window. They made no attempt to hide their identities. That was bad news; it probably meant they did not intend to let her go. They didn't even bother to close the door. If she could just work her feet loose, she could try to run for it. The thing was to buy time.

The heavyset dark-bearded man with a European accent hung a dim oily lamp from a hook on the wall, and rummaged through her day-pack. Thank the Goddess her notebook wasn't in it. Though it had been dark when she saw him, she would swear he was the same man who had been trying to coerce Charley back at the retreat.

In the dim light she could see that the one with a Texas accent had cowboy boots suspiciously like those described by the bag lady. Likely Texas was guilty of Sam's murder already; one more wouldn't matter to him.

The third man she recognized as J. Hijras, the Indian. He certainly got around. He took off her gag and said, solicitously, "No need to look so upset. Just tell us where Marta is. We want to talk to her."

Lynn had at least one thing to feel relieved about. If they were looking for Marta she was probably alive. "I don't know where she is. Why don't you ask the people at the retreat. They said they know."

The European snickered. "She got away from them the first day she was back here. We didn't even get a chance to make our case. Off to the villages to make trouble for us. Come on, we know you contracted to go trekking. She had to have contacted you, told you where to meet her."

Texas leaned forward impatiently. "Where is that bitch Marta? Goddamned trouble-making females! We know she brought you here to give us a hard time."

"I haven't seen Marta. Anyway how could a woman on a meditative retreat possibly give you any trouble?"

Texas snorted. "Quit trying to be clever; you can't fool us. You know perfectly well that she's been agitating the villagers against us. We know that's why you're here—to help her blow our cover."

"That's not true. I'm looking for her myself. She disappeared. The police still want her for murder. Sure I came here after that story. I have no idea what you do or who you are. But you must know where Marta is. You sent that kid in the leopard skin after me with her sari. How did you get that?"

The Indian said, "Easy. We found it in her room at the retreat. She left all such 'worldly' trappings behind when she left there. We know you've been in communication with her. We found this." He waved the torn blue envelope in front of her nose. They had been through her things in Sue's room!

They thought she was working with Marta, that she knew where Marta was. That had to mean that Marta wasn't just meditating in the mountains or visiting her mother's family. Was she hiding...from these men? What were they into that they were so afraid of her?

Texas spoke up again. "Too bad she had already left the address on this letter by the time we checked. But now that's not a problem since you'll tell us what you know."

There was silence for a moment. What could she say? They wouldn't believe the truth—that she really didn't know. Now was the time for a clever plan. Nothing entered her mind.

Texas spread Marta's sari over some crates set out the food on it in a rather fussy and orderly fashion, evenly spaced. While the others ate, he cleaned his boots and then his hands with water from a canteen. He even put all the trash in a plastic bag.

Mr. European ate in front of her noisily, then swung a bowl of food under her nose, making her flinch. He smiled. "No need to jump yet. We have saved the bloody part for later, some magic to help your memory."

"I don't have any idea where Marta is. If I did, I wouldn't have been hanging around at the retreat waiting for somebody to tell me where she is."

"We know you were in contact on your river trip. Someone saw her while you were there."

Lynn's heart thumped. Had Marta really been near when she visited the Baba? She should have tried to stay there. "If you know she is at the Baba's, why don't you go there?"

The Indian said, "Stupid female. She is no longer there."

"Why don't you ask the Baba to lead you to her?" Lynn asked sarcastically.

Texas snarled, "Shut up." Then he slapped her. She held her breath to stop the stinging.

The Indian put his hand on Texas' arm, but looked at Lynn with a slight smile. "No need for us to behave in such an uncivilized manner. If we are all interested in finding your friend Marta, there should be no problem."

If they believed she knew where Marta was, maybe they wouldn't kill her till they found out. "Did your friend with the leopard skin tell you that I spoke to Marta? Was he the one who said he saw her?"

"We should have waited, followed her when that Baba guy took her off trekking after Marta," Texas said.

The European snapped, "That fool doesn't know where Marta is and even if he did, he couldn't find his supper if it wasn't handed to him."

"But his followers...."

"You really want to take them on?"

Lynn said, "Look, you might as well just let me go. The Police are already looking for me. My editor had instructions to call them if she didn't hear from me tonight. I don't know where Marta is. I came here looking for her. The people at the retreat claim they know where she is—out on a meditating retreat."

The Indian frowned at Lynn. "Of course, once we have the information we want, we intend to put you on the morning bus to Kathmandu. We hoped you would be agreeable. We understand now you won't cooperate. We are prepared."

"What if I told you she has returned to the U.S.?" Silence. The three men waited. Finally she said, "I really don't know where Marta is."

The European said, "We know you were preparing for a trip into the mountains to meet with Marta. The Baba doesn't know where Marta is. Therefore you do. We have information that you were going to travel north into the mountains. You will tell us where you were going sooner or...later."

Texas moved fast and slapped her again. "We happen to know you were working together to try and interfere with our... business here. We know she came to see you to give you information. Otherwise you wouldn't be here trying to contact her; so why don't you just cooperate and we can all have a little get-together and work out our differences."

"If I did know, I wouldn't tell you."

He slapped her several more times. She was starting to feel sick. Maybe she could throw up on him.

He said, his face close to hers, "Remember Sam? He got too uppity too. Threatened to blow our cover. He'd be alive today if he'd been more cooperative."

An actual confession and she didn't have her tape recorder. But she wasn't going to survive to do anything with the information. Whatever she did or said, it was clear they intended to kill her.

The horror of the situation hit her full force and she had to control an attack of nausea and trembling. She had followed Marta to the ends of the earth, and now she felt as if she were about to fall off. The only thing that kept her from collapsing hopelessly was her overwhelming rage at herself for getting into this situation over a woman who she was sure now had never cared about her.

The Indian pushed Texas away. "There is no time for this now. We must move before dawn when the rituals begin." He retied the gag across Lynn's face. "You will stay here, suitably muffled, to listen to the cries of those animals sacrificed to the old gods. Through this hole you will be able to see the blood poured on the images. No one will hear your noises because of the cries of the animals and the noise of the crowd. Then your turn will come."

She watched them load some of the crates hurriedly onto the cart. What did those crates contain anyway that they were so heavy it took two men to lift them?

After they left, she worked on her bonds more, then, totally exhausted, dozed off. She was awakened by the loud noise of a crowd outside. Children's high voices shouting blended with the squeals and smell of animals. She tried to shout but the gag in her mouth muffled the sound. A frightened animal sound was all she could make and that blended with the noises outside.

The sunlight that came through cracks in the wooden door illuminated a spider web with a large spider not far from her face. It sat there unmoving as if to mock her. She scooted as far away as her bonds would let her. Was she was truly just another animal waiting for sacrifice. Braving the spider she worked her way to the door to look through the cracks.

Across a wide courtyard beyond the crowd they were slaughtering animals near a wall with the shapes of some of the gods carved into its reddened surface. He was right; she could smell the blood. A young goat was silenced as its throat was cut. Her blood was the same color. She tried to call out again but no one even turned their head. Did her captors really intend to kill her or was that just a threat to make her talk?

She got the gag out of her mouth and worked more diligently on her bonds using her teeth and finally freed her hands so that she could untie her feet. By that time the courtyard outside was dark, silent and deserted, no one to help. When it was finally clear she would never be able to get the door open, she vented her frustration by opening one of the crates. Carefully wrapped in paper and straw was an exquisite carved stone goddess much like those she had seen in some of the temples. Was it destined for Asia Imports? So they were smuggling religious relics out of the country; the import business their cover for illegal traffic in the national treasures of Nepal. Was this just a sideline to drug trade or their main business?

When her captors returned in the dark, she was waiting

behind the door and slipped through it while they lit the lamp. The trail outside the temple was narrow, steep and treacherous in the dark, but she managed to stumble and crawl over protruding roots and jagged rocks, the echo of their footsteps never far behind. She could see their flashlight flutter in the jungle around her like an insect in rhythm with their running feet. Her pursuers knew the windings and dangers of this path. At the bottom where the path ended in a steep bank above a stream, she huddled, exhausted, behind a tree. Their light caught her eyes, and she quickly rolled down into the stream. Bruised and disoriented, she couldn't get to her feet before they were upon her.

Mr. European was amused at the progress she had made and complimented her on her ingenuity as he dragged her back up the path.

Once back inside Texas glowered, silently rubbing mud from his boots with a rag while the other two tied her back up and dried off. Then the Indian asked, "Has your memory improved?"

Lynn shivered wet and exhausted. Her scratches still smarting from her scramble in the underbrush. She wondered if she would have told them if she did know where Marta was. Maybe she should make something up...they intended to kill her anyway. But she was too exhausted to respond.

The Indian said, a chilly flatness to his voice, "It's too bad that we are forced to resort to violence." Texas put away his cleaning rag and laughed, then he hit Lynn in the face. This time with closed fist. Silence—except that her ears were ringing. The European took a knife from his belt.

Lynn swallowed hard. Time for lies. "She's in a mountain village. I don't know how to get there."

"What is the name of it."

"I don't know."

This time the blow was to her stomach. She felt like throwing up, but now there was nothing there. She tried to remember what the map of the country looked like. "I think it was somewhere near the Tibetan border, near the new China road."

The European snorted. "And how was the Baba going to get you there? Fly?"

But Texas had relaxed now that she was talking. "That

makes sense. Marta could go over into Tibet with her buddies if she needed to." He got a map out of his bag and spread it out under the lamp, then held her head down over it. She could see the line that represented the road built through the mountains into Tibet. Fingers pinched into her neck, cutting off her breath.

"We'll know soon enough if you are lying. We have contacts in that area. They can check."

What was the chance that a random village in Nepal would be where Marta was? The Baba's guide had not told her where he was going to take her. The Tibetan border was very far away from the Terrai. Just as well. She picked a place, wondered how to pronounce the name written there, hoped the inhabitants wouldn't suffer too much at the hands of these three thugs if she named it. Still, she couldn't make herself say anything. The fingers tightened on her neck. She closed her eyes and pointed.

As she felt herself losing consciousness, she heard the European say, impatiently, "We haven't time for these games. If Marta is there our contacts find out. Now we need to get this one up the mountain long enough before dawn. I'm not taking chances on being seen by tourists on the road in daylight."

Texas said, "Why bother carting her around. Just cut her up here. There's enough blood on those stones...."

The Indian's voice was, cold, reasonable. "We do not need the trouble of a missing American here. There will be searches. She has to be found...recognizable."

When her mind cleared, Lynn prepared herself for another siege of questioning, but Texas was smiling at her. "We're turning you loose since you were so cooperative. Taking you to tourist country." He chuckled. She didn't believe him. But they untied her hands and offered her a share of their evening meal of soggy crackers, dry cheese and warm beer. She realized very soon that her beer had something added. No wonder it had tasted so awful. Too bad she had been so thirsty. She was aware of them watching her as she lost consciousness.

14

Damp and cool and dark. Her vision cleared slowly. After a moment, she realized the distant blurry lights she could see were stars. Something pricked her back, but she felt paralyzed. So groggy....

She tried to get up. So dizzy, such strange noises. Maybe just a few more minutes of rest. It would be light soon so she could see where she was. She fell back into unconsciousness.

She woke up again—light on the horizon—dawn. Her body felt stiff, abused. Suddenly she remembered her tormentors. What had they done to her while she was unconscious? She tried to move—check the damage. Her body was uniformly painful—stiff, bruised, but now she was not tied! She felt around tentatively with her hands—dirt and grass under her, the fabric of her pack behind her back, the trunk of a tree—with spines—a kapok tree.

She could just begin to see the hills around her through the morning mist. Still groggy—she heard something, a grinding sound from the other side of the tree. There was an animal smell. She stretched her head around and peered into the dimness.

A still dark shape just a few yards behind the tree. Christ! Terror brought her out of her stupor. A tiger was chewing on the remains of something that looked as if it once was a goat. She'd been propped up nearby with her day-pack on her back. The thugs hadn't expected her to wake up; they had set her out as tiger bait—to die. Lucky for her the tiger had left her for the second course. She remembered reading that some hotels left goats tied to posts to draw tigers for the tourists. So that's what Texas meant by "going to tourist country."

She controlled her panic and got up slowly in spite of her wildly beating heart. She climbed the kapok tree; fortunately, the spines where large and widely spaced. Still fighting the effects of the drug, her legs felt like lead pipes. She was glad for the adrenaline of fear that pushed her, and for the pain of the thorny trunk against her, keeping her awake.

Just as she reached a branch that she could pull herself up on, she felt a sharp pain, a tearing at her leg. The tiger had finally gotten around to her.

Swinging her weight over the branch, she hung there balanced on her stomach, trying to ignore the ache in her leg as well as the pain from the gouging spines.

Down below the tiger stood up on its hind legs, reaching for her face, and swatting at her like a cat with a mouse. It missed by a hair's breath. Lynn scrambled higher hoping that the cat was too full of goat to come up after her, or that women from South Dakota weren't to its taste.

In spite of the spines, she pulled herself into a sitting position on a branch as high up as she could get and clung there frozen with fear. The cat circled the tree several times, complaining loudly. Probably it wasn't hungry enough to make the effort, or it didn't like kapok spines. She prayed to the Goddess it was too lazy to come after her.

Finally it went back to its first meal.

Through the tree branches she watched the tawny-furred creature with dark stripes across its massive back as it chewed complacently on goat parts. Maybe after the sun decided to come all the way up the cat would go away.

She took her pocket knife and cut away the worst of the spines on her perch. There was plenty of time to wonder whether her captors expected the animal to just mangle her a little and terrify her. Maybe that had been their intent. She laughed at herself bitterly. Such charitable thinking. You don't leave somebody as tiger bait just to scare them.

And they hadn't left her pack out of concern for her welfare. They had wanted it to look like an unfortunate accident. Must have been to convince whomever might find her mangled remains that she was some stupid tourist who had gotten lost in the hills. She imagined the headlines:

Dim-witted Reporter, Wandering Aimlessly Through Jungle, Mangled by Tiger.

The painful and bloody wound the tiger had gashed in the back of her leg was already beginning to attract bugs. She looked through the pack; everything was there. In this case it had paid to be so thorough and cautious a person; there was actually a first aid box in her pack, complete with disinfectant. The band-aids were pitifully inadequate, but they covered the puncture wounds from the kapok spines. At least they had bled profusely. She wrapped a clean scarf around the oozing tiger wound and waited.

After a while, the cat strode off into the bush—no doubt to take a morning nap and digest its meal. She thanked the beast for its present disinterest.

No sign of tourists coming to watch the tiger eat. So much for that theory. From her perch all she could see were rice fields and trees. At length she climbed slowly down out of the tree. Better start moving before tiger gets hungry again.

How many hours down steep rocky trails? Were they trails or just breaks in the jungle? Here the hills were too steep for trees to take anchor. Each snap of a branch made her nervous, fearful that she would attract some other hungry beast. Nothing but a few birds high up in the trees overhead seemed to notice her. Then she heard the chatter of monkeys, and a mongoose startled her with its speed as it crossed her path.

Lots of trees with branches cut for fire wood and rice terraces clinging to the sides of the hills. Where were the people? She wished that she could have left a trail of bread crumbs or something like Hansel and Gretel. But the jungle creatures no doubt would already have consumed them.

She lay down to rest on the dusty clay at the edge of a rice field where the green shoots were just freshly planted. She munched on the last of the dry crackers from her pack and wondered once again if she dared drink the water that ran from the cracks in the clay wall. Better not. Stupid not to have water in her pack. She had been in too much of a hurry, trusting she would be back at the retreat and a safe supply of water. Maybe she would find an orange tree further down the hill. All she had left in her pack to eat was a few pieces of hard candy. She ate one and fell asleep in the shade of a castor plant dreaming of oranges.

She woke up, her leg throbbing, to look up into the brown eyes of a little girl, maybe six or seven, with a baby on her hip. Lynn was overjoyed to see both sympathy and curiosity in those wide brown eyes. When she sat up the girl backed away. Both children stood staring as if Lynn were a Martian. She pulled out the remains of a bag of hard candy and held out two of them. The girl hesitantly took them and stuffed them quickly inside her clothing. Lynn pointed to the wound on her leg and made noises that she hoped were like those of a tiger and motions indicating she needed help. The little girl giggled at her imitation, but pointed up the hill and started in that direction turning to see if Lynn followed her. She did.

A brown stone and clay house was just beyond the crest of the hill. A thin old woman was sweeping the courtyard. As they approached she looked up, then came toward them. The child said something pointing at Lynn's leg with its bloody scarf. The woman frowned and went inside the house. To get this far and then be ostracized. Lynn collapsed hopelessly in a shady corner of the courtyard while the children stood staring at her again. Were they waiting for her to die so they could rifle in her bag? She closed her eyes. She was too exhausted and discouraged to go further. After a little while the woman returned and Lynn felt a soft hand on her cheek. She opened her eyes and was offered a glass of hot tea and milk which she took gratefully.

Then the old woman squatted down next to her with a steaming mass of green in a clay pot and started to take off Lynn's improvised bandage. Lynn debated resisting but she had no strength left. People survived here without a hospital, didn't they? Packed on her leg, the green stuff looked sufficiently potent to cure anything, actually making the wound hurt less and keeping the bugs off. She fell asleep in the shade of the house.

She was gently shaken awake and opened her eyes to see the concerned face of a young man in spectacles. When he saw her eyes open, he sat back and smiled tentatively at her. In the dusk she could see that the other people of the household had returned from the fields, their mattocks still in hand, and were standing in a row staring at her. The young man in glasses was dressed in a neat white shirt, dark trousers, and sneakers rather than sandals or bare feet like the others.

He said hesitantly, as if not quite sure of his English, "Not good for foreign tourist to go into our hills alone. You are very far from trekking places. We see very few Westerners here. Government does not issue permits."

Lynn tried to stand up. Her head swam and she fell back against the building. Should she tell this man she had been kidnapped? Maybe he was in with the thugs that had kidnapped her. She didn't even know where she was.

He helped her stand. "We must take you to a place where you can get a bus to Kathmandu. You can find a Western doctor there."

They would put her on a bus to Kathmandu and she would lose her trail to Marta. He must have read the disappointment on her face because he said, "Not to worry. I am the school teacher here. I have been to University in India and understand. The medicine of the people here is very primitive—not for you."

She believed him. He really did want to help her. Perhaps as one of the few in these hills who spoke English, he would know of Marta? Westerners were rare, especially Westerners that were part Nepali and spoke the language.

"Thank you. I appreciate your help. I didn't know I was not allowed to come here. I came because I am looking for someone, another American, but one who is part Nepali. Her name is Marta Handley. She...."

The man looked startled; he exchanged words with some of the people standing nearby. He turned back to Lynn and said, "It is best you return to Kathmandu. We will make a bed for you tonight, and in the morning some of us will help you find the way back down to the road. If we leave early, you can catch the one bus that goes tomorrow."

Lynn touched his arm as he turned to leave. "Do you know of another American woman here, Marta, Marta Handley? I won't go back to Kathmandu until I find her."

Her leg began to throb as if to point out her foolishness. All the instruction she had heard about taking care with infections in the tropics echoed in her brain. But she braved it out, her heart pounding.

He stood staring at her over his glasses. At last he shrugged as if resigned to her intransigence. "I will tell those who might know where she is that you are here looking for her."

She let go of his arm thinking, how long would that take? Meanwhile her leg would be fermenting. Lose a leg to find Marta? But she didn't say anything.

"When you are stronger we will take you to the road where the bus comes. Perhaps tomorrow, perhaps the next day." He continued in response to her silence, "These people are poor. Your bus fare alone will cost more than they have."

She reached inside her shirt and into her money belt and handed him some money. He pocketed some of it and gave the rest to the old woman and her family. Then he turned to go.

The family shared their evening meal of lentil soup and rice with Lynn. After they ate, the old woman mixed another steaming batch of green glop to put on Lynn's gashes. She had to admit that it kept the mosquitoes off at least, and also that the wound did look better even in the dim light of the fire coals.

Dark comes suddenly in the tropics; in this village there was no electricity to hold back the demons of the night. One of the children helped her up the steep ladder into a corner of the sleeping loft. As she lay there in the dark Lynn found the sounds of people shifting and breathing themselves into their night's rest, comforting. The wounds did not hurt as much as they worried her. How long could she go without benefit of Western medicine? Was it even possible that she would heal without that intervention? The woman had applied her poultice, as if she had no doubts. Comforted by that thought, she finally dozed off dreaming that she was eating the crumbs from a cookie roof and the wicked witch who came out of the house was really Marta welcoming her home.

• • •

She was awakened by a shaft of daylight coming through the crack in the wall above her head and the noises of people already outside in the courtyard. In the dim light, she could see the room where she slept—a tiny loft. One corner of her loft was entirely taken up by a huge wooden chest, for food storage perhaps. Through the floor slats she could see the kitchen below with its cooking fire in the middle of the clay floor, the few cooking pots and spoons carefully hung on the wall.

She climbed painfully down the narrow ladder and found her way to the household toilet, the bank next to the river that the little girl had shown her the night before. Her leg was stiff but not too painful. The green paste, dry and flaky now, dropped off in spite of the stems with which it was tied.

In the courtyard her little friend was squatting next to a fire to escape the damp morning mist, feeding it with straw and popping corn one kernel at a time. Lynn joined her next to the fire and she offered Lynn a handful of dry corn. After a time, a woman gave Lynn a glass of hot tea and milk.

After most of the family left for their daily tasks, Lynn returned to her spot next to the hard clay wall, this time enjoying the warmth of the early morning sun. The little girl, again in charge of a baby sister, stayed to help her grandmother. The task for this morning seemed to be to make a pile of clay and cow dung in the middle of the hard clay courtyard.

After grandmother and granddaughter had assembled sufficient supplies, the old woman began to mix the ingredients slowly into a odorous red-brown mass. Slowly round and round, with her hand immersed up to the elbows, she stirred. More small children appeared and played mysterious games in the stuff. Then they plastered the walls of the house with it, repairing the places where cracks showed the rough stone bones underneath.

In the heat of the midday sun, the people returned from the fields to rest and share a meal of cold rice. This time the old lady smiled, because she could offer Lynn some fresh vegetable with her rice. And there was even a small sweet banana for dessert.

• • •

Lynn was asleep in the shade of a pile of rice straw when she was startled awake by voices. Jerking her head up, she looked anxiously into the courtyard. It was late afternoon and she could see the family was back from working in the fields. There was a group of people standing near the well. Had the thugs caught up with her? What would they use this time to kill her?

Then she looked closer. Was she still asleep? Her heart began to pound in her throat. Wasn't that Marta she saw squatting by the well with a glass of tea in her hands? Yes, it was really Marta in pants and shirt, her hair cropped, looking like a handsome boy. With her were several young men dressed as she was. They were talking quietly in Nepali as Lynn came up. Marta turned. There was a long dizzy moment as they exchanged glances, everything in slow motion. Was there anger in those dark eyes? She was sure that Marta could read the hurt and longing in her own eyes.

Marta came over to her. "We didn't want wake you. How are you feeling?" She put a hand on Lynn's forehead. "Not feverish that's good. Tiger wounds can be nasty."

Lynn was almost breathless with relief to have Marta there next to her.

Marta said something in Nepali to her companions, and then put an arm around Lynn leading her away from everyone through the field to the river bank and under the protective shade of a tree.

There were tears in Marta's eyes as she embraced Lynn, examined her leg carefully, touched her face, while Lynn told her what had happened.

Marta said, "We've been looking everywhere for you. You don't know how relieved I am that you are alive."

Lynn was surprised. "You knew I was in Nepal?"

"Yes, the Baba got word to me and now the authorities are looking for you too. That woman, Charley's mother, built a fire under them."

"Sue didn't leave?"

"Apparently not."

"How do you know so much, if you have been hiding out in the hills all this time?"

"Word got to us...I was afraid...."

"What did they think happened to me?"

"What Charley and Sue said to the authorities was that you probably got lost in the rhino park or something. The authorities assume you've gone trekking without telling anybody. Right now they are mostly concerned that you didn't apply for a trekking permit. People do it all the time. After all, you had your day-pack with you. They think you probably met up with some German tourists or something and went off with them. You'll show up wondering why everybody is making such a fuss. At least that's just what I'd like you to do."

"Charley knows who those guys are who kidnapped me. He warned me about them. He must have suspected that it was them."

"He did."

"Do you think they got him too?"

Marta smiled and shook her head. "I spoke with him by phone just this morning after I heard that you were here in this village. Or someone that sounded suspiciously like you."

Lynn took hold of Marta's arms wanting to shake her. "Why did you leave so suddenly without even a word? Why did you take off like that after promising me?..."

Marta pried her hands loose and squeezed Lynn's in her own. "I had to catch a plane. I didn't have time to go back to your apartment after the meeting. Jason left you my letter, got my things, then locked up your apartment."

Lynn pulled her hands away. "What letter? There was no letter, not even a note. Did you tell him to take the photos?"

"I don't know any thing about that. I'm sorry. It was Jason's idea to leave the letter; he had no reason not to. I suppose he was jealous. Several people knew you took pictures at that earlier meeting and were concerned about what you would write, but after your article was published, no more was said as far as I know."

"Then who did take them?"

"Somebody could have searched your room after I left to go to the meeting, I suppose. I gave Jason the key after we reached consensus on the issue of Asia Imports; that was about three o'clock. He was supposed to return the key with the letter at your apartment, then meet me at the airport."

"And what did the letter say that would have reassured me? I presume you intended to convince me not to try and help you."

Marta looked away. "At the meeting the leadership agreed not to cooperate with Asia Imports in any way—even legal importation of goods or crafts. I agreed not to talk to the police... and not to see you. I thought it would be easier if I left the country again, and I had to get back to warn people here in Nepal about the agreement... My letter explained all that."

"It wasn't there. And when I went to that retreat upstate and confronted him, he just said that you were meditating and didn't want to talk to me, and the Sister supported him."

"She doesn't know anything about any of this. She doesn't come to the management meetings. She leaves money matters to her staff."

Lynn couldn't keep the angry contempt out of her voice. "Protected from such mundane concerns as illegal drug trafficking?"

Marta looked down at her hands. "Kalimaya was never involved with drugs except to try and help people get free of them. Gruber and Allen claimed to sell jewelry and crafts and asked us to help with a new business in antiques."

"Importing national treasures of other countries is illegal."

"That's why, when I found out what they are doing, I got the Society to agree not to cooperate."

"I think Jason stole the pictures. I think he's been in on this all along. You know, Gruber and Allen were in those photos. Jason had his arms around their shoulders. In another photo he was shaking hands with them as if they had just struck a deal."

"I can't believe Jason was cooperating with them. I didn't know they were at that meeting. I've never even met them."

"They certainly know who you are. They were at the retreat saying they had joined the Society. They were looking for you at my apartment and they are looking for you now. And if Jason is so pure why didn't he leave me your note?"

"I don't know. Maybe to protect the Kalimayas from possible implication with drugs.... But I suppose it could mean that maybe he did intend more involvement with Asia Imports himself and was protecting his connection. But that doesn't implicate the Sister or the rest of the Society." She looked up at Lynn. "But you came here looking for me anyway, so not giving you my letter didn't keep you away."

Lynn's anger melted at the sad look in Marta's eyes. "Whatever the letter said, I think I might have tried to find you. The way the apartment was left...it looked like there might have been a struggle."

"There was, but it wasn't physical. I had to choose between my promise to you and my bargain with the leadership that they

163

would refuse all cooperation with Asia Imports on the condition that I leave the country and not talk to you or the police. How did you find out where to look for me?"

"I went upstate looking for you. I found Jason and the Sister. She told me you had never returned from your retreat in Nepal; I think she believed it. She showed me one of your letters. Later I found an address in the waste basket. I also read some of the letters she didn't plan for me to see. It gave me a clue about what you were up against. In any case the location of the retreat here is no secret. It was clear you were in trouble. Del found out that you had taken a plane."

"The police?"

"Yes, damn you. You tell me in a desperate voice that you have something important to say. And then, after promising me that you wouldn't leave without explaining, you disappear. What was I supposed to think?"

"I'm sorry; I trusted Jason to give the letter to you. He didn't know that I had made a promise to you—that not giving you the letter would make you think I was in trouble. I believed, still believe that he is loyal to the Society. I came to you for help because I thought that it was already too late to extricate the Society from the Asia Imports scheme. But at the meeting it seemed like I was wrong."

"You still haven't told me why Jason didn't leave the letter?"

"No doubt in his judgement it was better I just disappear. He already knew I was going to leave the Society. He wasn't the only one who was afraid for me to talk to you." She looked away for a moment. Then she said, "After the meeting, I felt that I didn't need to speak to the police because the leadership had agreed to have nothing further to do with the Asia Imports people. The meeting seemed to go the way I had hoped it would. I thought we had won our case. I didn't yet understand that those men would persist."

"Are you still convinced that the Society is pristine?"

"It's true that some people have let their greed and perhaps even their commitment to the success of the family lure them from the path. But just because there are a couple of crooks taking advantage of the devotees of Kali-ma, doesn't mean it is an evil organization. It's not where I have to put my energy right now, although there's a lot there that is wonderful and valuable. It can still be saved."

"Or in the words of my grandmother, a few bad apples don't spoil the whole damn bunch."

Marta sighed. "There is still no evidence that the Society is involved with the crooks that kidnapped you. I believed that the Society's agreement not to cooperate with Asia Imports would be enough."

"The men that kidnapped me tried to blackmail Charley into cooperating with them. Those men seemed to think they still had a fighting chance to get the Society involved."

Marta looked away. "I can only hope that won't happen."

"Your getting the agreement from the Kalimayas can't be the only reason they are after you now. If you have left the fold and are no longer in a position to organize the Kalimayas against them, why are they still so interested in finding you?"

Marta smiled. "Let's just say I and my friends here in Nepal are giving them a hard time in this country, making it difficult for them to operate in the villages. They depend on the poverty of the people here to recruit, both for their drug trade and the theft of treasures." She sighed. "And your kidnappers might find me, if I hang around here with you very long. That's why we've got to get you on a plane for home as fast as possible. What they tried to do to you was what they would like to do to me. It was a warning. I hate it that you should be the victim in the name of their message to us."

"Who is us?"

"There are a group of us who are dedicated to making political and social changes here. My mother and her family were mountain people, and, now, so am I, as much and as long as I can be. I've come back to my own place here, in Nepal, where I feel needed and where I want to be. I'm very sorry you got involved. I tried to avoid that. I hoped my letter would convince you to give up on me."

"Give up?" Lynn felt dizzy; was Marta saying she didn't care? "Then all those things you said that last day...were lies."

Marta took a deep breath. "No. It was as much because what I said was true that I couldn't see you again."

Lynn couldn't stand it any longer; she took Marta's hand,

whispering, "That doesn't make any sense to me. What is it that makes me still think your making love to me was just a way to get you a hiding place on your way back to your mission here?"

Marta looked at Lynn with tears beginning to form at the corners of her dark eyes. "You're right to be angry at me. I've treated you shabbily. But I meant every word." She looked away. "I had to make a choice. My loving you was a luxury, an indulgence that only ended up in hurting both of us. I am so sorry."

Lynn couldn't bear the tears. She put the hand she held next to her cheek. She wanted so badly to believe Marta now. "What matters to me is that I found you and you do care...and that we are together now."

Marta pulled her hand away. "But we can only have a few hours, then you must go back."

Again the hurt took over. "Not this time. I won't go back without you. You're a U.S. citizen. You've no business getting mixed up in all this. Those thugs tried to kill me. They won't stop till they get you too."

"You haven't been listening to me. You're lucky to be alive. I'm amazed that your wounds aren't festering. You can't stay here. You're a danger to the people in this village as well as to us." Marta looked at the ground. "The fewer people who know where I am, the safer we all are. That's why you have to leave now."

Lynn was furious. This woman was telling her what to do like a drill sergeant. Their whole relationship *had* been a lie, a farce, a hide-out for Marta-Tika while she was in the States. Who was this woman that called herself Tika and stood here giving orders? Lynn turned away to hide her own tears of anger. She would not just go quietly. There was a story here. At least she deserved to have that.

She swallowed her pain and said angrily, "And what about the woman you call the Sister; what is her role? Can you be so sure she is not behind this scheme to make money with Asia Imports?"

Marta shook her head. "I'm afraid, like women everywhere, she hasn't been in charge. She's what you accused me of being, a traditional woman, rather fatalistic. That makes her rather helpless. That's one reason why I finally left the Society. No matter what one's inner virtues, how long one meditates on goodness, one must still act in this world. Inner virtue won't save a mother dying of tuberculosis or a tribal tradition or solve the problem of erosion."

"Or make one's followers toe the line."

She smiled sadly. "It's ironic. You were right, you know, when you challenged the philosophy of the Sister's teachings. It's not possible to serve others successfully if one is not strong. I've learned this from the Tamang women here in the mountains. They're strong; independence is their tribal tradition as well as caring for others."

They sat in silence until a man's voice from behind them asked, "Did you get a good look at the men that kidnapped you?"

Lynn turned, startled. One of Marta's new companions—a handsome, dark-skinned young man stood behind them. Had he been listening to their conversation?

"Pardon for the interruption." He held out his hand to Lynn, European fashion and said, as if trying to bridge the awkward moment, "I am Joshua, a name I have because, you see, my mother was an Indian Christian. My father is Christian too, but a Sherpa. Like you from the Christian nations I do not belong to a traditional caste."

Marta explained, "Marrying outside your caste, class or tribe here is not accepted—one of the customs that is changing, if slowly."

Joshua stood politely, waiting for an answer to his question.

Lynn got up, her painful, private moment with Marta over. She had come to the end of her search. This was not the woman she had been looking for, not the woman she'd come to believe she was in love with. She answered Joshua, almost relieved for the interruption. "They certainly didn't bother to wear masks or anything."

"You would recognize them again?"

"Of course—"

Marta said urgently, "Lynn is going to Kathmandu as fast as we can get her on a bus." Then she turned away to hurry over to where her other companions were waiting. Joshua hurrying along beside her.

Lynn followed slowly, then stood at a distance while they

talked quietly. No doubt they were helping to arrange Lynn's future. The teacher listened to the discussion, then went to sit with the family.

Lynn went over to him and asked, "What are they arguing about?"

He looked at her for a moment, then reached in his pocket and took out a thin piece of paper. Lynn recognized it as a bus ticket. He handed it to her with some change. Then he whispered, "You must leave here as soon as possible. You are a danger to the people in this household and this community." He nodded toward Marta. "They are a danger, but they will leave if you do."

"But what are they saying about me?"

The man was silent for a long moment. Then he sighed and said, "They want you to help them trap those men that left you to the tiger. They need you to help identify them." He nodded. "What they want to do would be a good thing." He said something under his breath she didn't understand. Then said, "Those men are a scourge on the people. Tika and her friends would like to turn them over to the authorities in such a way that even the government has to recognize their evilness."

The reporter in Lynn came to the rescue. Now that would be a story! Lynn found herself walking over to Marta and her companions and saying to Marta, "If you won't come back to the States with me, at least I can help you here."

Marta pulled Lynn aside. There were tears in her eyes. "Why should you risk your life again?"

"Wait a minute; they tried to kill me! It would give me a lot of satisfaction to get them, not to mention the story I could write."

Marta still didn't say anything and Lynn continued, "Can't you see? It would be the news story of my life. Not only would I have an exclusive, world-wide, but I would get to tell the story, first person. It will be the making of my career."

Marta's eyes narrowed for a moment; then she walked away abruptly to talk to her companions. When she returned she said to Lynn, "Do you have any money left? We've got to get you some antibiotics if you're not going back now." Lynn reached for her money belt.

One of Marta's companions brought back antibiotics, dressed her wound, and declared her on the mend.

Then as soon as it was dark, they traveled in back of a closed truck that smelled of spices and sweat. It was one of those lumbering dusty vehicles, complete with Shiva portrait and dangling religious decor like the rest of the trucks that kept Nepal supplied with goods.

The truck stopped in the middle of nowhere and she and Marta got out. Lynn had no idea where they were. Once the truck's lights were gone, Lynn was overwhelmed by the completeness of the dark. Marta took her hand and they walked in silence along a narrow, steep mountain trail for what seemed a long time. Her leg ached while the voice from the back of her mind scolded peevishly. Could Marta really find her way with only the distant stars for light? All she could see was Marta's back, a shadow in the starlight.

And here she was again—right back into the frying pan. She could be on a bus safely on her way to Kathmandu and a hot bath. Her story of being kidnapped would be enough to keep Gale happy. She could be on her way home in a day. Wasn't it enough to get deceived by this woman once; she had to get involved in her crazy....

Finally they stopped next to another clay-walled house. This one had a new tin roof that reflected moonlight. Marta stood for a moment with her hands on the wall, resting.

"Where are we?" Lynn asked finally.

"It's better if you don't know right now." Marta was silent for a moment and then said quietly, "This is my mother's house. It was empty and in ruins when I came back. It was only in respect to my mother's family that it was not torn down or rebuilt by someone else. The villagers believed that my mother's family would come back."

"They must be very patient people."

"They were right. I'm here, and I've rebuilt it with their help."

Marta had made some improvements in the house which was very much like the one Lynn had stayed in earlier. One dirt-floored room with a fire pit in the middle and various pots, utensils, and stored food hanging from the rafters. Next to that room, a smaller storage space, and above, up a rickety ladder, a low loft for sleeping.

There was a small kerosene stove for heat and cooking, and one window with glass and a screen. Marta cooked them a meal of rice, dal baht, and watery vegetable soup. Lynn was amazed at how good the food tasted in spite of the way her leg throbbed after the difficult walk.

When she had finished eating Marta said to Lynn, "I've taken a vow at the temple in this village to stay and help my people." She smiled pensively. "I'm the American Tika to the people who want to change things here, a good luck charm. I hope I can help them make the transition from the old way of life that has always worked for them to a successful way of coping with the nasty technological society that is coming at them now from all directions..." She shook her head. "...Before they are destroyed by it."

She turned away. "People are losing more and more of their land to foreigners. The native people can't even find jobs in their own country, because they haven't yet gotten the skills to work in modernized society. And every day young girls are lost to the brothels of India, lured away by false promises of jobs. People here are so naive about the modern world and it's pitfalls." She looked at Lynn, her eyes clear and bright in the firelight. "I am the Tika, their prayer for good fortune."

"So do you consider yourself a revolutionary?"

Marta sighed, then smiled sadly, the tired lines of her face exaggerated by the yellow lamp light. "A rather extreme way of putting it. It's true I can't be resigned to the way things are." She smiled. "In that I am very much an American."

"Why didn't you tell me about this before. All those days you lived in my apartment. You must have known even then. Nancy said you were studying Nepalese."

"It happened very gradually. I came here to Nepal because the Kalimayas were building the retreat and the Sister needed someone to report back directly to her. At first I was just interested in finding the best way to build a spiritual retreat for our U.S. based membership. Then it didn't seem significant to me that my mother was born here. But like all Americans, I am a problem solver. When a worker was sick or needed to stay home because of a family crisis, I would go to the village to try and help for the sake of the project. Gradually I got more and more involved. There is so much. You have no idea."

"So now you will rescue people here instead of at the mission in Hartfield."

Marta shook her head. "You don't understand. Look at me. Who am I? Where is my center?" She touched the walls of the hut, tears in her eyes. "I've so much to learn. I'm not my mother, but I must find and nurture that part of me that is her. If I can offer something back, something that will help my people survive the twenty-first century with something of their own identity..."

She picked up her little oil lamp to study Lynn's face. "You're exhausted. Come on." She turned off the stove and the lamp and in the dark they climbed the rickety ladder to the loft in silence.

There was one patch of light where the moon shone through the edge of the rafters. Lynn pulled Marta over to it so that the moonlight showed every detail of her face. She studied this woman greedily. Her mind made snapshots in the moonlight—the motion of Marta's lashes, the shape of her face, the texture of her skin. She wanted to see and remember everything. The real Marta was with her now, hair cropped and sticking out over her ears like limp grass, her smooth olive skin burned by the tropical sun. She pulled Marta's hands into the spot of light. The fingernails were short and cracked and the palms calloused from working in the fields.

Marta's eyes reflected the moonlight with an amused curiosity. "What do you see?"

What Lynn saw was a beautiful woman, a woman she loved, even though she was just beginning to know her. From the reddening scratch on her cheek to the crinkle of laugh lines—the curve of her smooth sun-darkened cheek—the very special angle of the brow of her nose. She smoothed back the strands of hair and began to kiss the real Marta.

And the snapshot of moonlight moved slowly throughout the night, inch by inch as they made love slowly and exquisitely, napped and made love again.

15

From a tourist hotel, Lynn called Del Whitney whose voice, with its mix of relief and anger, sounded amazingly clear from half way around the world. "What the hell do you think you're doing, disappearing on me like that? I never thought I'd see the day, but you even got Gale in tears. Your parents have been on my back, calling every two hours. As if I wouldn't have called them if I'd heard from you." There was a pause. "I've already bought my ticket."

"You can't afford that."

"What the...I deserve a vacation. I'll celebrate your being alive and come anyway. Mom's taking the kids and I got time off from work. We'll play tourist together."

"I have to stay lost for a few more days. Tell everyone I'm OK, but that if they say a word to anybody till I call them, my life will be in danger. That should keep them quiet for a while.

Del still sounded annoyed. "Peter O'Hara is already there looking for you. I've got a ticket on the two o'clock plane, and I've already contacted the embassy and the local gendarmes."

"Good. Don't cancel any of it. I'm sort of caught in the middle of something here, but you don't have to write my obituary yet, although I have had a few bad moments. Where can I call you once you get here?"

"I'll be at the Hyatt. What'll I tell the U.S. authorities?"

"Get through to your connections. I just might have somebody they want. A US citizen heavy into illegal national treasures, maybe drugs—your murderer with the cowboy boots. Those importers Allen and Gruber are in it all the way—be prepared. "

"Jesus woman. Have you gone wacky in the bush? How'd you

do that all by yourself? You were supposed to contact us right away when you were on to something."

Lynn couldn't help laughing. "I am a little damaged, but my head is in very good shape, thanks. I just need your ever diligent policewoman help."

There was silence on the other end of the line, then Del said, "That Wyoming fellow and his mother, they contacted us when you disappeared."

"Charley. Charles Jackson."

"Yeh, that's the one. He gave us a lead on cowboy boots—one Merrill John Conners, a Texan. Worked for Asia Imports it seems, off and on. A long record in the drug trade. Lou Ellen Bailey has identified him. And—your Charley has agreed to testify that Merrill John tried to recruit him. He knew some things about Gruber and Allen too."

"You might want to check their warehouse, if they have one. The temple where Merrill John had me locked up was full of Nepalese national treasures. He bragged about murder when he thought I was tiger bait."

"Locked up?"

"And tied. But I got away. I'll fill you in when I see you."

There was a long silence then Del sighed. "OK, hon, leave it to me. See you soon."

Del had given her Peter's phone number in Kathmandu. Miraculously she found him in his room. "I am going to deliver some international crooks to the authorities, the crooks who have been giving the Kalimaya a bad name, not to mention murdering Sam Jenson. Merrill John Conners, a U.S. citizen is actually the one who probably wielded the murder weapon."

When he finally spoke, Peter sounded anxious. "How the hell are you going to deliver them?"

"I've got some help."

"What do you mean? It's quite a story if a bunch of locals got together to help you out. Who—"

"I can't divulge my sources."

"Come on now. You promised to share."

"I'd tell you if I could. I don't want to get them into trouble. They have enough to deal with already. I'll tell you when we have it set up."

"Tell me where you are at least."

" You'll have plenty of time to get there."

"I can't afford to waste my time sitting in a hotel."

" Fine, give me the number of the *Times*. I'm sure they would be happy to cooperate."

"OK, OK. Call tomorrow, same time."

● ● ●

In the dusty heat Lynn sat by the second story window of an ancient hotel on the road to the India-Nepal border watching as people poured out of the buses across the washed-out, lumpy pavement. Marta sat leaning against her, holding her hand, her dark head resting against the wooden window frame. Lynn wanted this moment, this touch forever.

This was the main rest stop on the route that public buses and trucks used from Kathmandu to India. Marta's friends had alerted her that a shipment was planned by Allen and Gruber.

But Lynn almost wished that the thugs would never show up. She and Marta could stay here, suspended in time, like the dust motes she was watching, caught in the warm air and turned orange in the late afternoon sun.

Would she be able to tell Marta when she did see the three men, knowing that would end their time together? But, of course, Marta would know. Marta would see it in her eyes.

Marta-Tika was a different woman, but still loved, now that some of the mystery was gone. If possible she loved this woman more than the Marta she had known before. The woman she held in her arms now was frank, open, talking enthusiastically about what she believed in. All energy and confidence, then quiet with a sad far away stare. Lynn had fallen in love all over again.

She savored each moment as if it were the last of her life. The tender care with which Marta bandaged her healing wounds, the sweet sound of her voice as she talked openly now about her childhood with a mother who never learned to speak English well. A mother who lit incense and put flowers in Marta's hair and a dab of rice on her forehead for good luck and was ashamed to go out of the house. She spoke of a mother who cooked strange food when no one else was home, so that the smell of it would be mixed with incense.

Marta's father in his own cold Puritanical way had loved her mother. But he also had been ashamed of her. His relatives would not visit. Marta went alone to her grandmother's house. She was treated kindly, but always there was that ghost of her mother in her Grandmother's eyes, when Marta's brown eyes were compared with her cousins' blue ones. Her mother had died when Marta was still too young to understand. Marta shared her sadness with Lynn.

Yet as Lynn listened to Marta, she felt truly happy. No matter that four dusty, whitewashed walls confined them. No matter the hard bed and gray sheets, the cold rice and overcooked vegetables. Lynn would remember forever each mark of the walls, the scarred tile of the floor, the hand-carved wood on the sills. And the silky touch and scent of Marta's cheek...as she leaned over to kiss the smooth velvet, one more time.

• • •

A bus destined to cross the border into India arrived for a rest stop. Marta sat up and Lynn leaned forward, concentrating, to watch through the dusty window as people got out.

She saw him, the same thick body, the same half sneer on his face—Gruber. This time he wore a light blue shirt, cotton trousers, and fashionable shoes with a leather jacket slung casually over one shoulder in deference to the heat. After him, came the Texan in blue jeans, Merrill John, with his five o'clock shadow and sweat spotting his white shirt. But his cowboy boots were carefully shined.

Two shy country girls in their village dress got off behind the two men. With them was...was it really him?—Leopard Boy, only now he was in tight jeans and a blue jean jacket. No sign of the Indian, Hijras, but three out of four—not bad.

Marta, reading Lynn's tension, squeezed her hand and said, "It's them isn't it?"

Lynn nodded and Marta quickly disappeared. Only moments later, Marta came back in the room hurriedly. "Those young girls were talking about jobs in India. Both of them are barely thirteen. I think we've caught our boys hustling minors into prostitution."

She hugged Lynn and began hurriedly to get her stuff together. "Thanks to you, those children will be saved from the Bombay whorehouses. We'll see they get home to their mothers suitably warned and chastised."

Lynn's heart was beating too hard. She was trying not to cry as Marta said, "You wait here for the next bus to Kathmandu. Give us a little time. There should be one through in about an hour."

"I'm coming with you," Lynn protested.

Marta stopped and came over to her, hands on her arms as if to restrain her. "You've done enough. I won't let you endanger yourself again for me...."

"You owe me this story. I need to be there. I am a reporter you know, and I am a witness. I told you before. There are people who want to be there when we deliver these thieves to the authorities. Right in front of me one of those guys admitted murdering Sam. I saw the treasures they have been stealing and they tried to kill me. I imagine Del already has extradition papers in the works for at least one of them."

Squeezing Lynn's arms, Marta said, "But they will recognize you."

Lynn cut a hunk of her hair with her pocket knife and stuck it under her nose with pieces of the transparent tape they had bought to bandage her leg. Marta burst out laughing and tried to grab her hand, as Lynn said, "I'll bet they know what you look like too. They've been after you a long time."

Marta pulled out a blond wig from her bag and it was Lynn's turn to laugh as she put on lipstick and a frilly blouse, a skirt and sandals.

They had to run to get on the bus in time, superficially a European couple on their way to a rafting trip in sunglasses and baseball hats. They hurried to their seats, bags and packages clutched near their faces.

Lynn watched the three men sitting from behind her sunglasses. They seemed nervous. Did they guess that something was up? A couple of Marta's mountain companions were on the bus too, sitting in the front next to the bus driver.

As the bus approached the border to India, Leopard Boy went up to talk to the driver and the bus pulled over, an unscheduled stop. The three were getting off the bus with the two girls. Marta and her two companions up front quietly followed them off the bus with Lynn trailing behind.

For a moment Lynn stood alone in the dark watching the bus pull away, her body frozen, wishing desperately she could run after it and get back on, safely on the way to India. Pure blind optimism kept her there, faith that Marta and her friends would be in control and not abandon her or end up dead. In the headlights of the disappearing bus she spotted a truck parked along the highway and figures running toward it.

Then it was dark again and all she could hear was scuffling. But in a moment Marta called out to her. "It's all right Lynn, we got them."

By the time Lynn got to the truck, she was relieved to see Marta holding a gun and a flashlight on Gruber and Merrill John and the missing Indian, J. Hijras, who had been driving the truck. Leopard Boy was gone. Marta shrugged and said to her questioning look, "We know who he is—which family he is from. After this there will be few places he can go."

Lynn found her hand being shaken formally if enthusiastically by Marta's two grinning Nepali companions after they searched the truck and found crates labeled as rice and food products but packed with antique images, ivory and gold ornaments stolen from shrines, as well as several kilos of heroin. "A real bonus," Marta said grinning too, tears of triumph in her eyes. "We've got them."

Merrill John, Gruber and Hijras were piled in a corner, trussed up like pigs. She and Marta and the two Tamang girls stayed in the back guarding them and the contraband while the other two drove.

While they bounced along rutted roads sitting on burlap bags in the back of the truck, Marta gave the two girls a lecture in Nepalese about the dangers of trusting strangers and Lynn dozed off with her head against a rice sack.

They had all agreed beforehand that if they managed to catch any of the crooks, it would be best to turn them over in such a way that the government could not ignore the evidence. That was Lynn's job—to make sure there was some press coverage. Now Lynn needed to alert Peter and Del. That meant they had to get to a phone.

Marta and Lynn were dropped outside a village that had a small hotel with a phone. Lynn called Peter in Kathmandu. "We did it. We've got three crooks and a truckload of contraband. Bring everybody. We need as much press as we can get to make sure that this doesn't get covered up."

Peter was outraged. "What do you mean? This is our story."

"It's too big. If you want to see me in one piece again, make sure that there is enough international coverage to embarrass anybody in the government who might try a cover-up. I don't want to end up tiger bait again."

"Let me get this clear. You expect me to bring the international press to an obscure government office in the mountains of Nepal at three o'clock in the morning."

"Right. It's not that far from where you are now. Before five a.m., or you'll miss everything including the sunrise."

"What've I got to lose? Just my reputation and my sleep."

Next she called Del at her hotel. "Call the Embassy. We got Sam's killer. Plus his buddies and a load of stuff."

"Merrill John?"

"I don't know about U.S. law and extradition procedures but he wears the fanciest pair of cowboy boots you ever saw."

Del was silent for a moment. "Don't worry kid I'm on my way."

"Good. Now I'll say good-bye. I've got to call my boss."

"It's OK, Lynn. I'll call Gale. I'll call everybody. You just get out of there alive."

16

Bumping along in the back of the truck after the two girls fell asleep, Lynn clung to Marta, trying not to hear her whispered good-byes. Had she come all the way to Nepal just to lose Marta again? How could Marta send her away, after all Lynn had done to prove how much she loved her?

No, this can't be happening, she was silently screaming when a sudden jolt sent her sprawling onto the floor. The truck had stopped. She felt Marta's arms around her in a final embrace then a cold steel object was placed in her hands, along with a loosely wrapped package.

Marta whispered, "Don't give this to anyone but the officer I described to you who is in charge. We've contacted him already, so he is well-informed. He will make a show of questioning you, but I think he won't give you any real trouble."

Through a mist of tears, Lynn could barely see Marta smiling sadly as she continued, "I trust with your experience as a reporter you can lie your way through this?"

Then, in the predawn dark, Marta and her companions and the two girls got out of the truck. Lynn could see that there was another truck waiting for them down the road at a small village.

Marta stood leaning at the open window. She wiped away the tears blinding Lynn's eyes with her shirttail and said, "Remember just keep going on this road. When you come to two hairpin turns in the road, you'll see it on the hillside ahead—some low buildings and a bunch of military tents surrounded by a fence. Don't try to park too close to the gate. There are armed guards. Park down the road, a bit outside the gate and walk them in so the guards can see who you are."

Overwhelmed with anger and sadness, Lynn put the truck in

gear and drove away not looking back. Marta was gone and gone with her were their moments together.

She tried to reason with herself that it mattered that she herself was alive and in one piece and, perhaps, would see Marta again. She reminded herself that she should be grateful that her father had taught her to shoot; at least she knew how to use the gun. But she had never tried to kill anything; doubted that she could shoot now, even these people who had beaten her, who had meant to kill her.

Golden light was just beginning to touch the highest peaks when the truck rounded a bend and Lynn could see ahead, barely visible in the pre-dawn light, a distant hillside of tents and a big square building—the military post. She parked the truck, picked up the gun and opened the back grabbing the end of the rope attached to the three tied-together thugs.

Then there was nothing but the sound of their feet on the pavement as they walked toward the outpost.

What a moment to see for the first time the glorious illumination of the highest mountains in the world, when all she could feel was her loss of Marta. The misty wonderland of white and gold mountains and green valleys didn't matter. Even the crooks on the other end of her tether didn't matter. What mattered was Marta gone.

No sign of Del and company at the post. Where were the hordes of international press?

Then up near the main building—moving silhouettes...a bunch of people running toward her. And behind them, was it a troop of soldiers? And was that Del in front?

Merrill John whispered something to the others. Then, all at once, they dove for the underbrush at the side of the road jerking the rope out of her hand. She followed them down the dusty bank shooting over their heads to stop them. Luckily the rope that tied them together got tangled in the underbrush stopping them long enough for her to catch up.

"OK, hold it there or the next bullet will be in your brain."

Merrill John and Gruber quit trying to get the rope untangled and turned to her, resigned, hands raised as high as the ropes and the brush would allow. The Indian squatted head and elbows on his knees. A sorry, dust-caked, trio. It gave her some satisfaction, now that the tables were turned, in spite of the hate in their eyes. She crouched above them, gun aimed carefully until the soldiers scrambled down the bank and took charge amidst the noise of cameras clicking above.

After she handed over the gun she looked up to see Del grinning at her.

And there was Peter too. He said as he helped her up the bank, "I said find the story not make it." Then she was surrounded by sleepy-eyed reporters. Her first international story and here she was in all her unwashed glory—dusty torn jeans, a streaked shirt with permanent sweat stains. She could hear her mother saying, "At least you could have combed your hair."

She gave her story to the reporters while following the soldiers and her captives. A Nepali man, not in uniform, met them on the path from the largest building, pulling a suit jacket over his crisp white shirt. The soldiers saluted him. Lynn mentioned the name Marta had given her.

He nodded and said in English, "You will come inside please and make a statement." The reporters tried to question him but he waved them away. She insisted that Del and Peter be allowed to come with her. Del showed him her identification and the papers she had from the U.S. government. Finally, he impatiently agreed to take her along too.

Once Lynn was sitting opposite him in his office, she handed him the package from her pack. "I left the truck with the rest of the contraband down the road. Your soldiers have charge of it by now."

He looked at the papers in the package. Read the statement of the two girls. Tapping his pen on the desk, he looked at Lynn. "Am I to believe that you captured these men by yourself, single handedly?"

"They held me captive for several days until finally I found my opportunity. I got one of their guns."

He looked annoyed. "How did you manage to tie them while you were holding the gun?"

"The girls helped me when they understood that these men were breaking the law, luring them away from their homes by false promises of work in India only to sell them into sexual slavery."

"And where are these girls now?"

"They returned to their village. That's in the statement."

"And you wrote this statement in Nepali language?"

"No the girls wrote it themselves."

"We will question them, see if their stories match yours. Those three kidnapped you, held you prisoner? Why?"

"There was another one, a Nepali citizen but he...escaped. They knew I was investigating their operation. That I might report about it in the U.S newspapers."

Del interrupted, handing him some sheets. "These are extradition papers for Merrill John Conners, a U.S. citizen wanted for drug trafficking, illegal importation, and murder. We also have evidence that Conners and another of the prisoners, H.C. Gruber, have been dealing in illegal importation of archeological treasure through a U. S. company, Asia Imports, owned by Gruber. The third man is an employee of Gruber, alias, J. Hijras. It's all in the statement."

He sighed, looked at her for a moment then he took the papers and lay them on his desk. "These will be dealt with in due order." He turned back to Lynn. "What I wish to know is how you managed to get here?"

"I drove— after I locked them up in the back."

He lay down his pen and leaned on his hand. "And why weren't you stopped at the check points?"

Lynn shrugged and smiled. "I guess they were out for tea. It was the middle of the night."

He smiled. "If we are to have a case against these men, we must approximate the truth."

"I'm just glad to be free of these monsters. Who knows what they were going to do to me."

"And the two girls?How did you talk to them?"

"They were brought in when I was still being held prisoner. I just remember waking up and finding the girls there. I guess they realized when they saw me tied up that they were in trouble too."

"Will they corroborate your story?"

Lynn shrugged.

Del spoke up. "Doesn't it seem in the interest of all of us to accept her story? This capture of international criminals will be heavily reported in the international press. I'm sure you realize the importance of this to your government. It seems to me my countrywoman here has done her part. The rest is up to you."

The official looked at Del for a long moment.

Peter, who had been very busy writing, looked up and said, "Meanwhile, we can tell the world that you are doing your part in dealing with the illegal trade in national treasures, not to mention the drug trade and the reprehensible traffic in human flesh."

The official leaned back in his chair staring at Peter. Then he said to Lynn, "Do you agree to testify to your story at a future time if necessary?" She nodded and he gave her a piece of paper to sign. Then he impatiently waved for them to leave. Peter stayed behind to take pictures.

Once outside, Lynn took a deep breath. "Thanks. I didn't know how I was going to get out of that one."

Del shrugged, smiling. "Remind me to ask you when I need a cover story to tell my children or my boss."

As they walked toward Del's rented car, the snowcapped peaks of the Himalayas were resplendent in the early morning sun, the valley below green-gold magic in the mist. Del stopped to look for a long moment then turned to Lynn. "Thank you."

"What for?"

She held out her arms to the horizon and turned three-hundred and sixty degrees. "This!"

17

A week later, Lynn and Del were sitting on a whitewashed stone wall on the top of a temple complex. Through the blue haze of cooking fires they could see all around them the green fields, red-roofed farm houses of the Kathmandu valley. In the distance huddled the ancient city buildings with their elaborate facades of carved wood. On one side of them was a white Buddhist dome with painted eyes. In front of them was one of the many small altars with an ancient stone goddess under her cloak of flower petals and rice paste.

A woman went by and placed an offering gently before the goddess, then turned and smiled at them and walked away.

It was Del's last day as a tourist. She sighed. "I wish the kids could be here. Not that Alita would do anything but claim to be bored and want to be home with her friends. I envy Marta—knowing where her mother came from, being able to go back there and find her family. My mother talks all the time about going to Africa once before she dies."

"You should go with her."

"Fat chance. I can't even save enough money to help the kids with college."

"Well you got here. Maybe we can find a crook to chase to Africa."

"Look, I'm not even sure I can get the department to pay for this trip. Let's not get carried away."

"Why not? You got Merrill John extradited. Two other crooks at least exposed. The Nepali government is on to Asia Imports."

Del turned to the little Goddess. "The kids' dad wants to take them to Africa—after all this time. He didn't do shit for them when they were smaller—now..." She shook her head. "...I suppose I should let them go before the place is completely ruined."

"Maybe you should take them—and your mom. He can pay for college."

Del smiled. "Good idea."

After Del left for home, Lynn got a call from Charley. He needed to talk to her. Could they meet for dinner?

He picked her up from her hotel in Kathmandu. He looked very different from the sunburned guru taking care of banana trees she had met at the retreat. He was dressed in an expensive cream linen suit with matching silk shirt, his only concession to his origins a string tie with a small tasteful silver clasp in the shape of an antelope.

They were in a tiny local restaurant going through a sumptuous plate of steamed Tibetan pastries stuffed with vegetables, dipped in a mixture of lemon and fresh hot peppers when he said, "I wanted you to know that the Kalimaya Society is no longer associated with illegal international trade in any way. Jason was implicated by Conners and was arrested. Singh has resigned from a leadership position and has returned to India. The Sister, of course, is not involved, never having questioned where the Society's resources were coming from. She left such worldly and mundane money matters to Jason and Singh."

Lynn chewed slowly on her delicious mouthful of savory hot food. Then she said skeptically. "Do you really believe that she knew nothing?"

"I prefer to believe it. I see no purpose in believing otherwise. The Society is important to me and a lot of other people. The work that Marta started will now become an essential part of the Society. Everyone agrees on that, so now there will be no opposition. I will personally see to it. We have set up an independent board of contributors and working members who will oversee the financial operations and make policy decisions on non-spiritual matters." He ate another pastry then reached into his coat pocket and handed Lynn an envelope.

It was from Sue. In it was a picture post card of their ranch and a letter:

Dear South Dakota;

When you get this I hope you are safely on your way home and away from the devils and demons in that infernal country. You gave us quite a turn. Didn't expect we'd see you again.

Now we do. On this card you will find our address with a small map of how to get there. I expect you to come visiting even though we don't have many crooks for you to chase. We do have lots of good home cooking, horses to ride and gorgeous mountain country. We got river rafting too. —Sue

Lynn handed Charley the note and he smiled as he read it. "She felt bad that we didn't take better care of you. When she saw that news photo of you alive and kicking, you don't know how relieved she was. I hope you'll take her up on the offer. She would be mighty pleased."

Lynn liked Sue and Charley. With Charley in charge there would be some hope that the Kalimaya Society could avoid illegal involvement in the future. She would go and see Sue and Charley at their ranch, next time she took a vacation.

● ● ●

Lynn waited impatiently in Kathmandu's stifling, crowded airport. Her plane would fly soon. She had done everything she could to get the message to Marta that she was leaving. Now Lynn finally had to admit that it was time to go home.

A figure in sea green silk hurried toward Lynn. Was it really Marta? Anger fought with love as she watched that familiar figure approach. Marta did not carry even a small suitcase.

Marta was breathless. "I couldn't let you go away without at least saying good-bye."

Until this moment, Lynn had not allowed herself to believe that Marta would not go home with her. Now she had to admit the truth. She would not see Marta again for a long time. She could not stop the flood of angry tears and the childish words. "I want to be with you. I love you. How can you let me leave? How can you put yourself in danger again?"

Marta didn't look at her. It was as if she wouldn't let herself hear Lynn's words. "I had this made for you." She held up a little figure on a silver chain. "Wear this image of Durga, to remind you of me and how much you mean to me. Then I will always be with you in spirit."

Lynn turned away in the crowded room to hide the tears. Marta led her away and they sat outside with a view toward the green fields of mustard and rice across the dusty road.

Marta said, "They say that at one time the gods were helpless against the demonic power that ruled the world. They went to Daughter of the Himalayas and asked her to rescue them. She reflected and then the many-armed Durga, the energy that governs the universe, manifested herself in the center of the lotus flower and was armed by all the gods. Sitting on the back of a lion, she went to fight the demons. Some say that during the battle with the demon Asuras, the Goddess of the annihilating power of time, Kali, energy of creation and dissolution, was manifested from Durga's forehead. Together they defeated all the demons."

Marta put the chain with the image of Kali-Durga around Lynn's neck. "I believe that it's now that the power of Durga and Kali must be called forth in my people so that they can defeat the demons that plague them."

"You aren't a goddess. You can't do that for them."

Marta smiled. "I know that now. Nor can you rescue me. But each of us can battle demons in our own way. Go home and be an arm of Durga for us. You are an American journalist. Use your freedom of speech, that arm that we don't yet have, to help us. You can work for us there in your own homeland and... ."

"I want to stay here with you, if you won't come back with me."

"Believe me, I won't let go of you now. One day we will be together again, each to celebrate our victory over our own demons."

Lynn sat for a while looking at Marta. Finally she said, trying to sound cheerful and not too bitter, "How about something a little less epic—how about I come back on a plane for a visit now and then."

Marta laughed. "Up in the mountains I forget there are things like planes sometimes. Yes, and I can come back—home, to the U.S. too...sometime. But for now there is too much work for me to do...here." Then for a few last moments, Lynn held Marta in her arms.